Alice forced herself to step into the room

Nick was sprawled across his bed, definitely asleep. There was no way he could have been prowling outside her room. Then what—?

"What the hell? Alice?" Nick sat up, the sheet falling to bare his chest.

"S-sorry. I—I didn't mean to wake you. I'll just be going now." Thoroughly humiliated, she hurried to the door. She turned the knob, but it didn't budge. She twisted and pulled and yanked and even offered up a whispered threat, but the door would not open.

Finally, reluctantly, she glanced at Nick. His expression was unreadable.

He indicated the bed with a nod. "Get in. Your teeth are chattering." She gaped at him, and he sighed. "Alice, that door isn't going to open until I explain something." When she didn't move, he continued, "I think Theora wants us to spend the night here…together."

Renee Roszel became a professional writer at the tender age of ten; her hometown newspaper paid her five dollars for a feature titled "My Pop Is Tops." However, her career didn't really take off until her two sons started school. She decided to try writing romance novels and hasn't looked back since. In the past few years, she was honored as the University of Oklahoma's Writer of the Year and was nominated for the prestigious RITA award.

Books by Renee Roszel

HARLEQUIN TEMPTATION
334—VALENTINE'S KNIGHT
378—UNWILLING WIFE
422—DEVIL TO PAY
468—NO MORE MR. NICE
483—SEX, LIES AND LEPRECHAUNS

GHOST WHISPERS
RENEE ROSZEL

Harlequin Books

TORONTO • NEW YORK • LONDON
AMSTERDAM • PARIS • SYDNEY • HAMBURG
STOCKHOLM • ATHENS • TOKYO • MILAN
MADRID • WARSAW • BUDAPEST • AUCKLAND

To Randall Albert Roszel,
a man too gentle for this earth

ISBN 0-373-25612-4

GHOST WHISPERS

1

NICK LIKED HER LIPS.

He knew everything about those lips—everything except how they felt. The idea of finding that out had crossed his mind more than once, but he'd always rejected the notion. Kissing the woman wasn't his job. Investigating her was.

He yawned. It was Wednesday. Hump day for those who worked a regular five-day week. Sometimes he envied the eight-to-five crowd. But mostly, he was glad he worked the crazy hours he did. It kept the memories at bay.

He'd just spent eight boring hours at the Department of Motor Vehicles doing background checks on employees for a corporate client. Tonight, however, wouldn't be boring. His evenings with her never were, though she had no idea he was there, watching her every move.

Nick liked watching her. She was a pretty woman, her bearing as subtle and sensual as her mouth. Long ago he'd vowed to never become involved with a woman, any woman, but he was still a fully functional male.

She was speaking now. Even looking through the passenger-side mirror, he could read her lips. She was

standing about ten feet behind his car, telling her landlord about her wedding plans. The date—November
20—was exactly five weeks away. Nick already knew
that. Silvanus had told him everything, even going so
far as to say he'd asked her to marry him in an unguarded moment. Silvanus had obviously regretted the
impulse because he'd hired Nick. "Better safe than
sorry," he'd said, handing Nick a check in advance for
his first week's surveillance. "She wouldn't be the first
girl to want me for my money."

Now she was laughing. Nick could hear the lilt of it;
the sound warmed him like strong, hot coffee on a chilly
stakeout.

From his vantage point, with his car facing the corner of her block, he couldn't see the other man's mouth
to read his lips. But it didn't matter. There was nothing
clandestine or underhanded about the exchange. It was
just a young woman chatting with her landlord on the
front steps of her Victorian apartment building. Nick
grinned, thinking that he wouldn't need the .38 he wore
at the small of his back tonight.

She laughed again, and Nick experienced a twinge
of guilt. He felt like a "staller," an unethical P.I. who
would feed a client information a little bit at a time,
drawing out the investigation as long as possible in order to charge a higher fee.

Actually, Nick had tried to tell Silvanus that a two-
week surveillance wasn't necessary, that the whole
thing should only take a couple of days. But his client

had insisted. He wanted both a thorough background check and an extended surveillance.

Dean Silvanus was one of Kansas City's most generous philanthropists. He was a little too slick-looking for Nick's tastes, with the quick smile of a political candidate and the poise of a television lawyer. But, if the guy wanted to make sure the woman he planned to marry was all she seemed to be—and was willing to pay for two weeks of surveillance—who was Nick to complain? The private investigation business was chicken one day and feathers the next. If Silvanus insisted on throwing his money away, that was his business.

Every time Nick started feeling guilty about taking his fee of two hundred a day plus expenses, he reminded himself that the next desperate woman who called him in tears, needing to hire somebody to find her child, kidnapped by a noncustodial father, he could afford to help. He liked helping people; he especially liked child recovery cases. Reuniting a parent and child made him happy—an emotion he wasn't quite convinced he deserved to feel.

Besides, he also had to eat. A good reason to still be tailing Alice Woods. After Silvanus's chauffeur had dropped her off, Nick had been there to take over, to observe and record where she went and who she saw. So far this evening, she'd walked to one particularly shifty-looking grocery mart. Now the sun was setting, and she was heading inside her apartment building, probably for the rest of the evening.

Since Silvanus was out of town, Nick had a feeling he'd be spending a long night in his car, watching her second-floor apartment while nothing at all depraved went on inside, unless, of course, she subscribed to X-rated cable.

Nick loosened his tie and sat back, his eyes never leaving the side mirror, gazing at lips with just enough lipstick to show that her mouth was perfect. During his investigation, he'd found that Alice-of-the-lilting-laugh had endured a lousy childhood, but had grown up to be one hell of a class act.

After a week and a half of surveillance and a background check that had started with her birth twenty-eight years ago, Nick had discovered the lady was as clean as Silvanus's fleet of white limousines.

He'd even employed the old honey-pot tactic, which meant throwing a handsome man into her path to see if she could be lured into a stranger's bed. The guy, Dave, was a friend of Nick's, a wannabe P.I. who worked part-time for Nick on just such jobs.

Dave looked like a blond Tom Cruise and continually bragged that no woman had ever said no to him. Nick smiled, recalling the frosty reception Dave's subtle, sexy line had gotten from Alice Woods. Dave had been wounded, angry, devastated. He'd felt like a failure. But Nick had assured him that he hadn't failed, the lady had simply passed a very rough test. Still, Nick wasn't sure if Dave would ever recover from the trouncing his ego had taken from the seemingly incorruptible Alice Woods.

As far as Nick and his growing report were concerned, she was clean and perfect, and Silvanus, that paranoid son of a bitch, would be damned lucky to get her.

Suddenly he heard a sound in the distance—the gunning of an engine and the squeal of tires. Some kid was headed for a speeding ticket.

He saw Alice frown, and he focused on her lips again, sensing a problem. "Oh, dear," Nick lip-read. "I forgot something, and the drugstore's closing. Maybe if I hurry..."

Glancing out his windshield he saw an elderly man locking up the drugstore across the street. At the same instant he heard Alice's clipped footsteps as she rushed past his car toward the corner, calling to the man and waving. He also heard something else. The speeding car. And it was louder now. From the sound, Nick could tell it was racing up the street toward the blind corner that Alice was headed for. Calling out to the store proprietor the way she was, it was obvious she didn't hear the car coming.

Instinctively, he launched himself out of the car, leaped across the hood, and reached the curb just as she stepped off. Grabbing her protectively against him, he fell backward onto the sidewalk. With a grunt of pain, he took the brunt of the impact on his bad shoulder.

Groceries rolled and bounced into the street where she would have been. A big can of tomato juice thudded loudly against the grillwork of the souped-up Buick that had been speeding down the side street. Nick looked up in time to see the can split open and splatter its thick, red contents over the windshield, then bounce off the hood and clatter into the middle of the road.

It didn't surprise him that the teenage driver sped on, disappearing into the dusk. Before he did, however, Nick was able to get the first two numbers of his license. Then, suddenly, his view was blocked when the woman who'd been lying on his chest lifted her head and shook it.

"Hell," he gritted, belatedly realizing what he'd done. In a split second he'd gone from anonymous investigator to being the damned cavalry. What was he going to do now—slide out from under her and slip back into oblivion? She was looking down at him, her eyes wide with shock and confusion, but she seemed lucid. With her face so close to his, he knew she'd recognize him if she saw him tailing her now. People had a tendency to remember other people once they'd straddled each other's privates.

She swallowed, running a shaky hand through hair as black as coal. "Are—are you okay?" she asked. That surprised him. Her first thoughts were for him. He wondered if she'd have been so concerned if she'd known why he was there in the first place.

Even though he'd taken a giant leap toward screwing up the surveillance, he had to grin. "Not really. I feel like I should have bought you dinner first."

She appeared momentarily bewildered, then frowned, looking downward. When she saw that her legs were splayed across his hips and that her short, wrap skirt showed a risqué amount of leg, hose and garter belt, her cheeks pinkened.

That charming flush of embarrassment affected Nick in a way he never would have expected. Straddling him the way she was, Alice couldn't help but notice his appreciative male reaction. And clearly she did, for her gaze rocketed to his. Next to those sexy lips of hers, he liked her eyes the best. They were remarkable; large and hazel-colored, with golden rims. And right now, they were more than a little scandalized. He doubted that she'd ever found herself in a position like this before. But, he decided wryly, she could have, if she'd wanted to. Anybody with lips and eyes like that could heat up male hormones without a speck of effort—suddenly he could understand why Dean Silvanus had proposed to her with such uncharacteristic haste.

Nick recovered himself, at least mentally, and rose up on an elbow. "Apparently, I'm fine," he murmured, unable to deny the obvious.

His movement seemed to jar her from her stunned paralysis, and she scrambled off his lap.

Then Nick stood, wincing at the throbbing pain in his shoulder—the shoulder that had already sustained enough damage. With effort, he put the pain from his mind as he leaned down to offer her his left hand. Marveling that her cheeks were still flushed, he wondered what the hell Silvanus doubted about this woman's character. He'd never seen anyone more genuine in his life. With his fingers outstretched, he said, "Let me help you."

She shook her head, and her shoulder-length black hair caught the streetlight and was illuminated dramatically. "I'm okay, really. . . ." She got to her feet and surveyed the street, which was now strewn with her groceries.

The chubby landlord had rescued a tin of coffee and a plastic bag containing celery. A loaf of Italian bread was smashed flat, as were two soup cans. The tomato juice had sloshed all over, making the street look like the scene of a bloody hit-and-run. "Oh, my," she breathed, possibly realizing for the first time how close she'd come to being killed. She whirled to stare at Nick. "You—you saved me," she cried softly, her face going ashen. "How can I ever repay you?"

He gritted his teeth, but managed what he hoped was a nonchalant grin. "I was just in the right place at the right time," he lied. He was being paid good money to spy on her, by a man she loved—a man who didn't quite trust her. But that was the last bit of news she needed to hear right now.

Her landlord came over and handed her what he'd managed to salvage. "You okay, Alice?" he asked, his round face ruddy with concern.

"I'm fine, thanks, Sandy," she murmured. "I know you've got a date. You go on."

Sandy, a flaccid, balding man around forty, gave Nick a suspicious once-over, then turned back to Alice. When she offered him a weak smile of encouragement and said, "Good night," he nodded, seemingly satisfied, and shuffled off.

Alice turned to Nick, her golden-brown eyes glimmering. He could tell that shock was settling in. Impulsively, he took her arm. "Maybe you ought to sit down."

She didn't protest this time. "Maybe I should," she whispered, indicating the corner café. After a waitress led them to a back booth, Nick ordered coffee for them both, while Alice drew a handkerchief from her purse and dabbed at a splash of tomato juice on her cheek.

He watched silently. He'd never been this close to her, never smelled her perfume. It reminded him of baby powder—light and flowery and quietly wholesome. It suited her, he decided.

So this was Alice Marie Woods, up close and personal—the little girl other kids used to call the Dummy's Daughter. He'd found out that she'd been raised by her father, a deaf, antisocial janitor, in a windowless basement apartment in a decaying section of town. She'd been neglected by today's standards, but she'd proved to be strong and resilient, having worked her way through college to become a teacher for deaf children.

Nick had an urge to take those pale, shaky hands in his and tell her he admired her, not only for her spirit and courage, but for what she'd done for those kids—until, at Silvanus's urging, she'd quit her job. As far as Nick was concerned, Silvanus had lost points for that show of selfishness. Having been deaf as a child, Nick knew firsthand the loneliness and pain—

She said something, interrupting his thoughts. "What?" he asked, as the waitress brought their coffee.

She poured cream into hers. "I asked you how you managed to react so quickly out there. I didn't see you at all, and then suddenly you appeared—like magic."

He shrugged. He couldn't tell her he'd been reading her lips and knew she was heading into the street. Didn't want to go into his own history of being a cop, trained to react with a cop's instincts. There was too much sadness connected to that subject. "Let's just say I'm gifted that way."

She sipped her coffee, peering at him. "Are you saying you're psychic?" She sounded skeptical.

He laughed. "If I were psychic, I'd have told you not to go into the damned street in the first place."

She smiled, and Nick sensed she was recovering from her fright. He took a swig of his coffee. It scalded his mouth. But the wince that touched his brow wasn't caused by the burning coffee. No, it was a direct result of the realization that he was being an idiot. This wouldn't do, this fraternizing with—well, not the enemy—the subject. Silvanus would be thrilled to see this chummy little scene. "I'd better go," he said, getting up. "Now that I'm sure you're going to live."

She looked startled. "Already? I don't even know your name."

He smiled down at her, with a practiced, fake grin, since inside he was irritated with himself. He should have expected this. She'd be the type who'd want to make friends with the person she perceived as a hero.

"The name's Nick," he said, wondering what was the matter with him, giving her his real name, though most of his business associates knew him as Dominic. Reaching out, he offered his hand. "Nicholas Street," he added, for lack of inspiration. Out the window he could see the sewer grate—he was lucky he hadn't blurted out, "Nick Sewer."

He was sure as hell not going to tell her his real last name. Falcon Investigative Services was well enough known in Kansas City, as was the name Dominic Falcon. She didn't look dumb. Nice, but not dumb. If she happened to see him again in the next couple of days, she'd put two and two together and know he was tailing her. "And you?" he queried politely, as if he didn't know everything about her except the details of the night she lost her virginity.

She took his hand in hers. He could feel the strength in her hand, no doubt the result of all the signing for the deaf she'd done. "Alice Woods," she said. "I'm very grateful for what you did today, Nick."

He withdrew his hand slowly, reluctance washing through him. "Well, Alice," he said, tossing a couple of dollars on the table. "I've got to go."

"Do you live around here?" she asked, quickly rising, and Nick was sure that she wanted to bring him home-baked cookies for his good deed, which was so quaint it made him feel like even more of a louse.

Shaking his head, he turned away. "Just passing through." Then he headed for the door and out of her life—at least as far as she would ever know.

FRIDAY EVENING, Nick's report was complete. Either Alice Woods was as pure as the driven snow, or she was so good at hiding her bad side, she'd scammed him. He'd bet his eight years of experience as a Kansas City cop and four years as a P.I., that she was exactly what she appeared to be—an honest woman with a good heart. He wanted to end his surveillance report with the words, "She's too damned good for you, Silvanus," but decided it might not be the most professional way to handle a well-paying client whose only fault, it seemed, was to have had the need to investigate Alice Woods in the first place.

He got up from his desk and went out into the reception area. Without preamble, he handed an audiotape to his part-time secretary/receptionist, Myra Johnson, a mahogany-skinned beauty who was going to graduate from law school all too soon. She'd be around until May, but after that, he'd be losing one sharp employee. The legal world would be gaining a clever, scrappy advocate for justice. But he really didn't like the idea.

"My, here's the Woods report. Can you type it up by Monday noon?"

She took the tape in long, slender fingers free of jewelry and gave it a frowning glance. "Sure, Nick, but it's all a waste." She turned it over in her hand. "I told you when I saw her picture she was the type of woman who'd die before she'd hurt a bug." She tapped the cassette on her desk for emphasis. "I bet you ten bucks she'd rescue a spider and put it outside before she'd kill it."

"I wouldn't doubt it." He frowned at himself. The comment had sounded melancholy. Absently, he shoved his hands into his slacks pockets, searching his feelings. Was he actually depressed that his time with Alice Woods was over?

Myra glanced at him, her black eyes keenly penetrating. "Don't tell me you liked the lady. You? Mr. Woman?-What's-a-woman? Falcon?"

Nick shoved the foolish idea to the back of his mind and lifted a warning brow, his signal to lay off his personal life.

Since Myra had seen that look before, she merely shrugged and turned back to her computer.

"Did Luke return my call?" he asked.

She shook her head. "I'll—"

The office door opened and a smiling gorilla of a man in a damp trench coat barreled in. "Nope. I decided to drop by and see how the other half lives."

"Other half of what?" Myra asked tartly. "If it weren't for me dropping by half days to give this monk with a gun some human contact, he'd be a complete loner."

Luke laughed, but Nick could detect a note of brittleness. The gruff old cop knew why Nick was no longer on the force and why he lived his life alone. Luke also knew that Nick never discussed the reasons for either with anyone. There was no way for Myra to know she was opening painful wounds when she teased Nick that way. She'd only come to work for him two years ago—

long after his torturous physical rehabilitation had ended. And except for a residual weakness in his right arm, Nick seemed as normal as anyone; he just wasn't normal enough to be on the police force.

Clearing his throat, Luke indicated Nick's private office. "Got your call, but thought I'd drop up here since I was cashing my paycheck, anyway. Convenient, you havin' your office above a bank."

Myra laughed. "All the better for prospective clients to pretend they're making a deposit rather than hiring a P.I. to catch their cheating husbands," she chimed in.

Nick slung his good arm around Luke's boulder-size shoulders. "Come on in here, old man. It's been a while."

They went into Nick's office where Luke took a seat on the low-slung beige couch beside the door, avoiding the less substantial saber-legged chairs that faced Nick's desk.

"Hell," Luke groused. "Place even looks like a damned bank."

Nick leaned forward, grinning. "Why not? Every-thing in it's owned by one."

The cop grunted. "Don't jerk me around. From what I hear you're one of the top private dicks in town. You gotta be rakin' it in."

Nick shrugged, sitting back. "Easy come, easy go."

Luke scowled, his expression turning speculative. "You still doing gratis child-recovery stuff?"

Nick chuckled, but didn't reply. Luke's nose for the truth was as good as ever. "So, what about the skip trace I need? Can you handle it for me?"

Luke scratched his chin, and Nick could hear the rasp of the five o'clock shadow under the man's sausagelike fingers.

Finally, Luke shook his head. "Been working on something on my own time. Got a feeling, but no proof. Captain thinks I'm crazy, but if I'm right, it's gonna be a big bust. Anyway," he said, crossing his boat-size chukkas, "one of the other guys, Hank Boone, has been looking for some off-duty work. Got a kid starting college. Said he'd handle it for you."

"Send him around early Monday morning." Nick absently eyed the abstract oil painting on the wall above Luke's head. It was the only boldly colorful thing in the room. He didn't much care for it. Didn't much care for anything. "So," he queried, his curiosity aroused, "who's this slimeball the chief doesn't want you to touch?"

There was a long pause, and Nick glanced at his friend again.

"Hell, Falcon, I got nothin' but my nose twitching yet."

"Your nose has come through when all the technology in creation has crapped out. What have you got?"

"Falcon," Luke said dourly, his eyes narrowing, "what's your take on Dean Silvanus?"

The hair bristled on the back of Nick's neck. "What the hell...? You're not saying you think Mr. Do-Gooder's dirty."

Luke seemed to sag. He exhaled loudly, dropping his head back against the wall to stare up at the ceiling. "Yeah, I know how it sounds. And I gotta be careful who I spill this to, because that oily-smiling pillar of society has friends in high places. But, there's something screwy in his operation. I got me a pretty reliable snitch." He ran both hands through his thinning hair. "Could just be a bitter ex-employee trying to stir up trouble for Silvanus, but I got a feeling— Me and my nose..."

Nick had grown alert. "You know Silvanus hired me to check out his fiancée?"

Luke nodded, looking at his friend. "Yeah. I been keeping tabs on the old weasel in my off-duty hours for almost a month. Saw you two at dinner." He grinned sheepishly. "Scared the liver outa me before I found out what he wanted with you. For half a minute I thought—" He cut himself off. "Naw, not really. Just jolted me to see you hooked up with him."

Nick frowned. "How sure are you about Silvanus?"

Luke reached inside his coat for a pack of cigarettes, then stopped. "You still got that no-smoking rule?"

Nick waved off the question. "Go ahead, kill yourself if you want. Just tell me how sure you are about Silvanus."

Luke shoved the cigarettes back into his pocket. "As sure as I can get without a blood-oath confession. And that slick bastard isn't likely to hand me one. Why do you care?" He looked sharply at his friend. "Hey. You don't look so good, man."

"It's the woman," Nick muttered.

"The fiancée you been checking out?" Luke asked. "She'd better have a thick hide on her, 'cause if I'm right—and I am—when this hits the fan the media's gonna have a field day. Anybody close to Silvanus'll get smeared with his stink."

A strange, cold anger flooded through Nick. To maintain control, he took in a deep, quick breath, then released it, breathing slowly out. It didn't help. Impatiently he toyed with a pencil. "Yeah, it'll be tough on her," he admitted, unable to shake from his brain the picture of a courageous little girl with golden-haloed eyes—the Dummy's Daughter. Dammit. She'd already borne too much humiliation in her life. Was she going to have to go through even more?

The drawn-out silence was broken by the sharp crack of a splintering pencil.

ALICE CHECKED HER WATCH. It was half past eight. Time had really slipped away. She shook her head self-consciously, realizing her mind had slid back to thoughts of her sad-eyed rescuer once again. Nick Street, her very own reluctant hero. She smiled at the memory. What a nice man. She was sorry she hadn't been able to really thank him for what he'd done. At least write him a nice note or bake him some cookies. She supposed he was married, and no doubt his wife wouldn't appreciate his receiving a gushy letter from a strange woman. Even from the little time she'd spent with Nick, she knew he was a special person. His wife was one lucky woman.

She glanced at her watch again, frowning as her mind returned to reality. She was getting hungry. Dean was very late for their dinner date. Of course, he was a busy man, and he'd been late before, but never this late. She got up and paced across her modest living room to ease her tension and caught her reflection in the mirror over the fake hearth.

She looked fine, she told herself, though she wasn't crazy about black clothing. It reminded her of dark places and unhappy times. But Dean liked her in black, and she had to admit, it set off the pearls. She fingered the long, double strand he'd given her as an engagement present last month. It was truly breathtaking.

She continually found herself awed by her good luck. How a man as important and well-respected as Dean Silvanus could have given her a second look, she couldn't imagine. He was so powerful and strong and generous—and interested in everything she had to say. She'd never felt so treasured in her life. She'd never felt treasured at all, to be perfectly honest. So Dean's doting attention was like something out of a dream.

The buzzer sounded and she jumped, then inhaled with relief. He was finally here. With a bright smile, she hurried to the door and flung it open, only to have her greeting die on her lips. It wasn't Dean, after all, but a stocky man in a well-tailored suit. Mr. Evangeline. One of Dean's business associates. Though the man had the flawless skin of a baby and a pleasantly soft-featured face, he had the icy stare of a thug. Alice had never been comfortable around him and always avoided direct eye contact. "Hello," she said, searching past him to look for her fiancé. "Has—has Dean been delayed?"

Mr. Evangeline shook his head. "I have a message from him. May I come in?" He asked the question in a tone that made it sound like an order.

With only the slightest hesitation, she stepped aside, allowing him to enter. He was almost constantly with Dean, and she knew he was completely loyal to his boss. There was no reason not to trust him. Still, she took a couple of protective steps backward. She supposed wealthy men like Dean needed bodyguard types like Mr. Evangeline. It was just one of the trials of living in today's dangerous society. She managed a weak smile. "Would you care for a cup of coffee, Mr. Evangeline?" She silently hoped he'd decline.

He shook his head. "The message is," he stated abruptly, "Mr. Silvanus is breaking off his engagement to you as of now. You can keep the ring and necklace, but don't try to contact him."

Alice heard him. Every word. But nothing registered. It was as though he'd suddenly switched to some foreign language she couldn't understand. She blinked, realizing he was turning to go. In shock, she clutched at his sleeve. "Wait!" Dashing forward, she blocked his exit. "What are you saying? Why is he doing this?"

Evangeline's cold eyes met hers and seemed to grow colder. "He's had an unfavorable report on you."

"Report?" she echoed, barely breathing. "I—I don't understand."

Evangeline gave her a thoroughly disinterested look. "The background check he had done on you confirmed that you're seeing another man. A convicted felon named Sam 'The Scam' Bosso. A bunko artist and two-time loser." The husky man smiled thinly. "Women like you have tried to get Mr. Silvanus's money before. Luckily, the boss decided to have you checked out."

"Checked out?" she echoed, dazed. His crazy accusations were bouncing off her shock-dulled mind and she was grasping little of what he was saying.

Evangeline snorted. "Investigated, bitch." He chuckled evilly. "Gotta give you credit. You were damn good. But Dominic Falcon found you out." Yanking the expensive fabric of his sleeve from her grip, he muscled by her and slammed the door in her face.

Alice couldn't move, could only stare for a long time. Her dismay was so complete, she couldn't even put together a coherent thought.

Finally, when her brain began to clear and function again, she found herself filled with indignant, white-hot fury. Who was Dominic Falcon? And why was he lying about her?

2

Nick barely missed running into Alice outside his office the next morning. He always took the fire stairs at the end of the corridor, because he was usually in too much of a hurry to bother waiting for the elevator. He'd loped halfway down to the first-floor landing when he realized he'd forgotten his cap with the ponytail attached—one of the disguises he used when he went to blue-collar areas on a case. He simply shed his suit coat and tie, slipped on a Kansas City Royals jacket and the baseball cap, and blended in.

Swinging around, he took the stairs two at a time. He'd just started to open the fire door when he saw Alice marching off the elevator toward his office. Stopping dead in his tracks, he held the door open only a crack.

She was wearing a thigh-length white V-neck sweater, black leggings and ankle boots. Her gleaming hair was pulled away from her face and tied at her nape. She looked casual and cuddly, as though she were ready to curl up before an autumn fire and purr in some lucky man's arms—except for her curled fists, stiff stride and pinched face, which shattered any such illusion. Looking more closely, he noticed that her eyes were red and puffy, and he felt a twinge of guilt. She'd obviously spent a good part of last night crying.

No doubt she was here to call him the lying bastard he was. He had an urge to go out there and take her in his arms and reassure her, tell her that what he'd done had been for her own good. But he couldn't. He'd struggled long and hard before he'd made the decision to falsify his report, and to waver now would negate his hard-fought decision. So he stood rooted, with guilt searing his belly.

She tried the knob. It didn't budge. Then she rattled it. Nick could see the frustration stiffen her spine further as she gave the door a slug with the heel of her hand and muttered an anathema that sent him to the deepest pit of hell. He grimaced, leaning tiredly against the cool cement wall of the stairwell. Myra would be furious with him. She'd typed up the real report only to have Nick secretly discard it and concoct one of his own. Or Luke, the straightest of cops, who probably wouldn't say anything—just give him a stern, disapproving look.

And, his brain nagged, if his falsification of an investigation was ever discovered, the state attorney general's office would take a dim view, too. He could be brought up on criminal fraud charges, not to mention losing his private investigator's license. Nick was risking his reputation, his livelihood—everything he cared about—with this lie, as well as possibly ruining Alice Woods's chance at happiness.

What the hell was his problem? Why was he interfering in this woman's life? He made it a rule never to get involved with clients. Hell, he didn't get involved with anybody. So why was he involving himself in her life when there wasn't a shred of actual proof that Silvanus was anything but a do-gooder?

Nick had been up for two nights straight, figuring out how to make his doctored report sound reasonable. He only hoped he'd bought enough time for Luke to gather the evidence needed to prove that allegations of racketeering and underworld connections against Silvanus were true. It was a sucker's bet at best; the odds were a hundred to one that Nick's ploy would work, but at this point it was a done deal.

Alice gave the office door a kick, then spun around and leaned against it heavily. She ran both hands through her hair and cursed under her breath.

Nick had never heard her swear before today, and he smiled in spite of himself. Her spirit and temper made him curiously proud of her. Clearly she wasn't as helplessly sweet as he'd thought. He supposed she'd had to develop some crust, dealing with the taunts and slights she'd received as a child. "Good for you, darlin'" he mouthed.

She pulled a notepad and a pen from her shoulder bag. It took her only seconds to scribble something on it before she ripped off the page and slid it under his office door. Then she stalked off to catch the elevator as it disgorged a mother and son on their way to the dental office next to Nick's. As soon as the elevator doors closed, Nick went to his office and unlocked it, grabbing up the note. "Mr. Falcon," it read. "My name is Alice Woods, and I'll see you in court!"

He crumpled the page and slipped it into his suit-coat pocket. Forcing her threat from his mind, he retrieved his baseball cap with ponytail. This morning he was being paid to locate a bail jumper. There was nothing else he could do but go on working—until Alice Woods's lawsuit ruined him.

ALICE WAS SITTING in the back booth of the coffee shop next to her apartment, feeling utterly broken and confused. She'd only just faced the fact that what had happened to her since Mr. Evangeline's visit last night wasn't a crazy nightmare. Suddenly she had no fiancé, no job, and a soiled reputation.

She'd spent most of the day butting her head against brick walls. She'd called Dean several times but had been frostily informed that he was "unavailable." She'd taken a taxi to his walled mansion, but had been turned away—a humiliating experience, considering that just days before, the gate guard had cheerily accepted a tin of fudge she'd made for him. Today he'd been stony-faced, if a bit uncomfortable, when he'd said Mr. Silvanus was not receiving guests.

It had been no better at Dominic Falcon's office: closed tighter than a childproof aspirin bottle. She'd only been able to leave him an angrily scribbled note. Then, halfway back to her apartment, she'd realized she had practically no money, so she'd got out of the cab and waited thirty minutes in the rain for a bus.

She'd spent every one of those thirty minutes wondering why she'd let Dean talk her into selling her car. He'd *said* she'd have unlimited use of his limousines, and that he'd ordered her a fancy German car as a wedding gift. So why, he'd insisted, should she keep her old clunker? *Why, indeed?* she groused inwardly. Maybe, in case he decided to toss her aside like an empty caviar jar! At least she'd been able to depend on her car.

She was livid with Silvanus for having her checked out by a private investigator in the first place—and then without even hearing her side, acting like a coldblooded weenie who couldn't break off their engagement face-to-face. And speaking of livid—she was almost grateful she hadn't seen Dominic Falcon in person. She might have committed vicious murder right there— using whatever instrument of destruction was handy. Dominic Falcon was very lucky he'd slept late! The lazy, lying bum!

She took a sip of her coffee and looked up with a wan smile as a middle-aged woman in a tidy pink uniform refilled her mug and gave her a pitying look. Alice could well imagine why. She'd changed out of her wet things, but her hair hung limply around her shoulders. And though she'd cried herself dry, she was sure her face showed the ravages of a sleepless, desolate night.

She checked her watch. The crystal was fogged, and she realized that her wait in the rain had ruined it. *Fitting*, she lamented silently. *Why shouldn't everything be ruined?* She gazed despondently at the clock on the wall behind the counter. Four-thirty. She supposed she should be hungry; she hadn't eaten all day. With a sigh, she caught the waitress's eye. "Nellie, do you have any beef stew this evening?" she asked.

The waitress grinned and licked the tip of her pencil before writing the order down. "Sure, hon. Glad you decided to eat. Ya look sorta puny."

Alice turned away, fearing Nellie's sympathy would bring a fresh welling of tears. Swallowing, she turned back, focusing on Nellie's scrawny neck, and managed a tremulous smile. "I think a little stew would settle my stomach."

The older woman scribbled. "Maybe some hot tea, too, hon? That's soothing when you're feeling sickly."

Not really caring what went into her stomach, Alice nodded, dropping her gaze to her mug.

Nellie hesitated, probably wanting to ask what was wrong. Apparently she decided not to butt in, because after a three- or four-second pause, she moved away with a squeak of her soft-soled loafers.

Alice took a sip of coffee. She pictured Dean in her mind. Tall and slender, with silver-haired good looks, he was not only wealthy but highly respected in the community. So, when he'd told her she really shouldn't keep her teaching job, she'd quit. He'd assured her she would do more good as his wife, helping various charities and causes, than she ever would teaching a few "damaged" kids. She hadn't liked that word, but had let it go.

Her stew and her hot tea came, and she took a couple of absent bites. Though she knew it was excellent, it tasted like soggy cardboard to her. Still, after a time, the food and tea began to warm her in spite of her deadened spirits, and something else stirred to life within her.

Mixed with her anger and hurt she felt an odd sense of liberation, but couldn't quite understand why. She thought of Dean again. The charismatic philanthropist who'd doted on her, treasured her, and—a little voice whispered a strange word and she shivered. Why was her brain trying to sneak in the word *smothered?* That simply wasn't true. He'd been devoted, perhaps overly protective, but not smothering.

It was true that Dean was a man accustomed to getting what he wanted. He'd made her cringe once or twice in restaurants by making a scene if the wine wasn't up to his standards. And she'd seen him grow unreasonable if anyone read the paper before he saw it. Still, he'd never been a tyrant. He'd made suggestions meant to help her fit into his social circle. After all, he was twelve years her senior, admired by thousands of people. Who was she to doubt his wisdom?

But he made you quit a job you loved. That had bothered her quite a bit, but she'd said nothing at the time. She now realized she'd denied her unhappiness, but with his heartless rejection last night, her resentment had surfaced as fully formed stomach-churning bitterness.

How dare he make me quit my job! And how dare he make me sell my car? she protested inwardly. *I loved that job and that car. Now look at me, stranded and alone.* She gritted her teeth. *How dare he tell me my clothes were "too young!"* He'd insisted on tons and tons of basic black. She really loathed black. "I never saw it until now," she said aloud, staring, unseeing, into her stew, "but you have a lot of gall!"

"Maybe I'd better order the pancakes, then," came a deep voice from nearby.

Alice started, her glance darting to see Nick Street's handsome face. Discovering him towering beside her table was a shock, but an oddly pleasant one. On the tall side of six feet, he was wearing a button-down shirt, a loosened tie and a damp trench coat. His thick brown hair, his face and his sooty lashes all glistened with droplets of rain. There was something so riveting, so sexy about his obvious masculinity, that all her anger left her.

Green eyes that she remembered as amused yet somehow distant, were watchful as he surveyed her face. His features were sharp and strong, with an inherent sensuality that she knew could be used to great advantage if getting a woman into bed was his goal. But now his face was somber, his firm lips drawn down, and a muscle was pulsing in his lean jaw. She had a feeling he wasn't sure he was welcome, and she couldn't imagine why. She smiled up at him, feeling strangely tongue-tied. "Uh, hello . . ." She stretched out a hand in greeting. "This is a surprise, Nick. I thought you were just passing through the other day."

His glance slid to her hand, and after a brief hesitation, he engulfed her fingers in his, half grinning, although the expression held no humor. "I pass through a lot," he offered quietly. "Didn't know if you'd remember me."

Alice hadn't realized how cold her fingers were until he took them in his. Though he'd come inside from a blowing rain, his skin radiated a comforting heat that she didn't want to relinquish. "How could I forget you," she assured, perhaps too quickly, and was surprised to notice that her pulse was racing. She supposed she could attribute her reaction to her chaotic state of mind. Her emotions had taken quite a beating in the past twenty-four hours.

"May I sit down?" he asked.

"Actually, I'd appreciate a little uncomplicated chatter," she admitted before she could stop herself. It upset her that she'd told him that. It upset her, further, that her tone had been so melancholy.

Usually she didn't encourage strange men. Of course, this particular man *had* saved her life—which unfortunately was now in a shambles. But that wasn't his fault. Besides, he didn't have the look of a jerk on the make. To be honest, he looked as though he wished he was somewhere else.

Well, no matter what the reason, he was here, and she did owe him. If giving him a little conversation during dinner on a rainy evening was what he wanted, then it was the least she could do.

His half smile faded as he shrugged off his trench coat and sat on the bench opposite her. She registered the fact that he wore a conservative navy suit that emphasized extremely broad shoulders. It wasn't a custom-made suit like Dean always wore, but well made and classic, nevertheless.

His clothes told her he was in some sort of conservative business. His eyes told her he was intelligent, wary and not very happy. As Nellie scurried over to give him a menu, Alice decided that Nick Street's unexpected appearance would be the perfect diversion from her troubles. Maybe she could pass a little time finding out why this intelligent, wary, not very happy businessman had come back here.

Why in the hell did I come back? Nick demanded inwardly, astounded at himself. After he'd finished his work for the day, he hadn't been able to go home and just forget about—everything. Not this time. A raven-haired woman with provocative lips haunted his thoughts. So here he was, slipping back into her life.

His need to see her again made him furious. Damn Alice Woods for making him feel! He didn't want to feel anymore. He wanted control, to stay detached. So why was he failing this time? Why was he feeling guilt for what he'd done? He'd helped ruin marriages before. Of course, they'd been marriages that were already falling apart. That was all in a day's work.

He exhaled tiredly. This time it had been different. He'd used deception to ruin her chance to marry a wealthy, respected man, and for no damned good reason. It was his guilt that had driven him back here.

So, just what did he think he was going to do? He had no idea, but he didn't seem to be getting up and heading for the door.

She was staring at him, perplexed. Could he blame her? "You don't recommend the stew?" he asked, giving the menu a cursory glance, trying to make conversation.

"The stew's very good," she said, sounding confused. "What do you mean, I don't recommend it?"

"You were shouting at it when I came in," he commented dryly.

Her expression grew pained. "Oh, that . . ."

He felt like a jerk, which wasn't new for him. "I've heard it can help to tell your troubles to a stranger." The words had come out without conscious thought, and he gritted his teeth against a curse.

She peered at him, clearly reluctant to share her distress. "What makes you think I have any troubles?"

He leaned back, weary all the way to his soul, much too aware that he was the cause of her troubles. "Didn't I tell you?" he murmured. "I'm gifted that way."

She sat back, too, looking drained. He could see she was vacillating between the horror of telling a complete stranger everything, and the desire to do exactly that. He remained quiet. Maybe she'd oblige him by refusing his offer to listen, and he could get up and walk out of her life.

"I—I don't—"

She was interrupted by Nellie's return. "What can I get you, sir?" she asked, popping her gum loudly.

He handed her the menu. "Stew and coffee," he said, his gaze never leaving Alice's face.

"Yes, sir."

Once they were alone, Alice started to speak, then stopped and shook her head. "Why are you doing this?" Leaning forward in a conspiratorial manner, she rested her hands on the table. "Are you in some sort of lodge that makes you do a good deed every week? Don't you remember, I was last week's good deed?" A telltale shimmer in her eyes made him flinch. "Isn't there some rule against helping the same person over and over?"

He experienced a surge of compassion for her and smiled, this time meaning it. "Luckily, that rule's been repealed." He placed his hands on the table, and when his fingers grazed hers, she pulled her hands into her lap. Damn! The woman was hard to help—probably harder to help than to seduce.

When she met his gaze again, her eyes were filled with a compelling mixture of torment and warmth, and Nick suddenly realized why he'd returned. Alice Woods was like a brave little flower blooming in a crack in the sidewalk. Someone as honest and caring as she was was so rare in his world of liars and cheats, he couldn't just step on her and forget it. He had to know she'd be okay.

"Why don't you tell me about it, Alice?" he urged, this time meaning it.

She swallowed and nervously began to toy with her spoon. "You're very nice, Nick."

His mood darkened, but he managed to retain his grin. "I'm one in a million," he kidded. "So tell me why you were angry at your stew."

Her lips curled upward at his humorous remark. "I don't know why I'm doing this." She sighed. "I guess I'm not right in the head, today. But since you've already ordered dinner, and I'm not in any hurry to go out in the rain . . ."

His stew and coffee came, but he ignored them; he hadn't come here to eat. "I'm listening." He was curious to hear her thoughts about the great and powerful Dean Silvanus and all that had happened to her since he'd turned in his fake report. To be truthful, however, he had no burning desire to hear her declare her loathing for a certain private investigator.

With raw hurt glistening in her eyes, she began tonelessly, "I was dumped last night . . . by Dean Silvanus. Have you heard of him?" Her voice was mechanical, as though she was trying to keep herself emotionally distant.

Nick cleared his throat and nodded. "I've heard of him. Go on."

She lowered her gaze to her lap. "We met six months ago when he donated some money to the school for deaf kids where I taught. He was awarded the Citizen of the Year plaque at a reception that day and was talking to a group of well-wishers when he turned in my direction and our eyes met...." She laughed nervously. "I know it sounds like a cliché. You know, that 'across a crowded room' silliness. But that's the way it was." Her glance momentarily met his, then darted away. "He just walked away from the group he'd been with and came straight to me and said, 'My God—'" She stopped abruptly, flushing.

Nick didn't need to hear the next part. Silvanus had told him exactly what had happened. He'd walked over to Alice and said, 'My God, you're lovely.' Nick experienced another surge of dislike for Silvanus. Still trying to continue the pretense, he coaxed, "My God— what?"

She set down her teacup. "Nothing," she insisted softly. "Anyway, he was so charming and impetuous, I guess I was—was swept off my feet." Unconsciously she began to twist her hands together. "After that, everything was a sweet blur. Suddenly he was escorting me to the theater and the opera, to gala banquets where he was being honored. Once, we even went to a cocktail party at the governor's mansion. I felt like, uh ..."

"Cinderella?" He'd just bet she did. To have the governor call her by her first name—that would have to be an amazing, dizzying climb for someone who'd spent much of her life ignored or sneered at.

Her thoughts must have been moving along a similar path, for she grimaced and touched her mouth as though she'd bitten the inside of her lip. "Yes, Cinderella would be about right, I guess." She dabbed her napkin at her lip where she'd drawn blood. After a long pause, she went on, "Then last month he asked me to marry him." She took a deep breath, her smile brittle. "I thought I'd fallen into a happily-ever-after fairy tale. He was so attentive, so caring, and such a powerful man. I did feel like Cinderella—and it felt good." She eyed him guardedly. "Am I boring you yet?"

"I'll let you know when I'm bored," he said, frankly. "So the man was a prince?"

Her brows drew together. "Well, nobody's perfect. On the downside, I regretted having to quit my job. But Dean said that as the fiancée—and soon-to-be wife—of a prominent man like him, I'd have 'duties.' He actually said, 'important social duties.'" Her features hardening, she added more tersely, "I loved working with those kids. Once this thing's straightened out, Dean and I are going to have to talk about that."

Nick shouldn't have been surprised by her remark. Had he thought Alice would just walk away from the man she loved without a fight? Didn't he already know Dean would take her back as soon as the lies in his report were discovered? He supposed it was his cue to ask what happened to cause the breakup. "So, why did Silvanus dump you?"

Her skin pinkened and her eyes were suddenly sparking and reproachful. "You won't believe *this*, but some jerk named Dominic Falcon—he *calls* himself a private investigator—told Dean I was just after his money. That I was actually seeing some con artist. Which is so totally crazy it should be funny!" she cried, shaking her head. "But, nobody seems to be laughing."

"Why would anybody do that to you?"

"The guy's either a moron or he's unbalanced," she muttered, her fingers clenched in a death grip around the edge of the table. "I can't understand it. Dean won't talk to me, and that Falcon idiot wasn't in his office. I'm going to get to the bottom of it, believe me! This afternoon I hired a private investigator of my own. He'll prove the report was false. Then I can sue that incompetent ass for everything he has!"

"Who did you hire?" Nick asked, trying to sound only mildly curious.

"Mort Hobart. I heard he was one of the best."

Nick nodded. "I've heard that, too." In truth, Mort was Nick's fiercest competitor. He'd dig up the lie if anybody could. Nick knew he'd better take diversionary action, and quickly. Luckily, he had a snitch he could ask to sidetrack Hobart from learning the truth too soon.

He knew his report about Alice would be hard to check, since Sam "The Scam" Bosso, the ex-con he'd picked to be Alice's illicit lover, was making himself scarce because of heavy debts. Nick's only prayer was that, between his snitch's slyness and Scam's ability to hide, Hobart would have difficulty smelling out the lie. Nick just hoped that Hobart wouldn't find out the truth until after Luke built his case against Silvanus.

"Nick?" Alice asked. "Are you okay? You went a little pale."

The grin he flashed was as much a thing of fiction as his report on her had been. "I was listening," he said. "You were saying you need a job." Something unpleasant niggled at his brain, but he ignored it.

She sighed sadly. "I don't know what I'm going to do. It's October—that's mid-semester. Not a good time to be looking for a teaching position."

Faced with the dejection in those gold-rimmed eyes, he maintained his virtuous expression with difficulty. A job. Hell, he knew of a job. *No!* he argued with himself. *No way. You just came here to make sure she was okay. No way are you getting more involved! You don't owe her anything. When you leave this table tonight, you're out of it!*

"I've got to do something," she went on. "I prefer working with the deaf, but—but, I think I'd like to get away from Kansas City for a while. To think about ... everything." She shook her head helplessly. "Without a job, though, I can't afford to go anywhere."

The bothersome notion prowled around in Nick's brain, refusing to be banished. "Damn," he muttered.

"What?" Alice asked. "What's wrong?"

He gave an impatient shrug, frowning. "Nothing. Go on with what you were saying."

She ran a hand through her damp hair, tucking a tendril behind one ear. "It's just that I'm broke. Dean's flunky told me I could keep my ring and a necklace Dean had given me, but I mailed them back today." Sighing, she continued, "That was probably stupid, but

I couldn't keep them after—well, you know. What's even more stupid is that a couple of weeks ago I took the money I got from the sale of my car and bought Dean a wedding gift."

"Can't you return it?"

She laughed forlornly. "It's an oil painting of Dean's bulldog, Nixon." She eyed heaven. "Lucky me. I'm the proud owner of a fourteen-hundred-dollar picture of a dog whose major form of entertainment was chewing up my purses."

Nick closed his eyes. This wasn't going well. He could just see her being evicted from her apartment, a suitcase clutched in one hand and a painting of a jowly canine in the other. Okay, so maybe he did owe her . . . a little. "I know about a job," he finally said. With a vague sense of disbelief, he listened to himself go on, "I have a deaf friend who needs a companion. To be honest, she's a witch and can't keep help long. She'd grab at the chance to have you stay a month while she advertises for someone more permanent." Well aware that he was completely certifiable, he offered, "Since no buses run that deep into the Ozarks, I can drive you there. I've meant to visit her for a long time. Giving you a ride would be a good excuse to take a few days of vacation."

"Oh, my," Alice breathed. "I can't believe it."

Nick glanced at her face, realizing his aversion for the whole idea had forced him to turn away even if it hadn't made him shut his mouth. She was smiling at him, her expression so full of gratitude, she looked as though she thought he was a saint. The sight was like a punch in the gut.

"Why are you doing this?" she asked. "Do you feel responsible for me because you saved my life?"

Resentment that her smile could affect him caused anger to rise within him. And he hated the fact that she'd placed a trusting hand over his. He'd done nothing to the woman but spy on her, lie about her and deceive her. It had been his manipulations that had put her in such an awful position. He was responsible, all right. Not for saving her life, but for causing her problems.

What he wanted most in the world was to be able to walk away. What he wanted least in the world was to care.

But, damn it—he did.

3

ALICE COULDN'T BELIEVE she was sitting in a car with a virtual stranger heading through a heavily wooded, remote area of the Ozark Mountains. The man beside her could be a serial killer.... But Alice wasn't really worried—for some inexplicable reason, she trusted him.

She glanced over at Nick Street, her rescuer, her confidant, her friend, though he seemed reluctant to accept either gratitude or friendship. He was concentrating on the winding mountain road, as silent and solemn as he'd been for much of the three-hour drive. Alice would have given more than a penny for his thoughts, if she'd had the money. She thought doing good deeds was supposed to make a person happy, but Nick appeared far from that. His firm lips were set in a grim line, and a muscle was jumping in his jaw. He was clearly preoccupied by some plaguing thought, and she was eaten up with curiosity about what such a good-hearted person might have to be so gloomy about.

The serial-killer idea flitted through her brain again, but she squelched it, knowing it was ridiculous. Nick was one of the most honorable people she'd ever met. She supposed she'd been watching too many movies-of-the-week.

She examined his profile. Remote as his expression was, she liked that face and felt almost guilty about how attracted to him she was—especially since she was in love with another man. Most likely it was just hero worship. Yes, that had to be it.

Since he was concentrating on the road, she knew he wouldn't be aware that she was watching him, so she stared unabashedly. There was innate strength there, and the five-o'clock shadow he now sported made him seem daring, enigmatic—less like a businessman and more like a spy.

The notion jarred her a little, but she ignored it, scanning his thick hair. It was the color of rich maple syrup and came just to the top of his crisp, white collar. She wondered why, even on vacation, he wore a suit. Mob guys did that, didn't they? She gave herself a mental shake. If only he'd talked more about himself. Not knowing much about him gave her imagination license to fill in the missing details. To help put an end to her paranoid thoughts, she voiced one of the questions she'd wanted to ask ever since he'd told her about this job three days ago. "What exactly do you do for a living, Nick?"

He glanced her way, frowned, then returned his gaze to the twisting roadway. His hesitation and disgruntled glance made her stomach clench. *Not the mob, please!*

"I'm a traveling salesman for Locksmith Supplies of America," he said at last.

"Really?" She felt a rush of surprised relief. "You look more like a—a stockbroker."

A brow rose and fell in mute cynicism, but he made no comment.

"I guess you never worry about forgetting your keys. After all, you carry around a sample case full of lock picks," she joked, hoping to jar him from his dark musings and get him to open up.

He grinned mildly. "Unless you've locked your sample case inside the house along with your keys."

She laughed, her mood strangely light, considering her present circumstances. His smile had an unorthodox effect on her senses. "Not you." She touched his arm fondly. "I haven't known you long, but I'd bet my last dime you're not a man who'd do anything as stupid as that."

He lost his grin. "Everybody does stupid things."

She was sorry he'd grown serious again, but his remark about stupid things reminded her of something else, something about that stupid P.I., Dominic Falcon. "I talked to Mort Hobart this morning. You know, the private investigator I hired," she said, drawing a fleeting glance from Nick.

"Oh?"

"Yes. He told me Falcon has a good reputation in the business. Can you believe that?"

Nick pursed his lips. "What else did he say?"

"Well..." Her cheeks grew hot. "Because the jerk does have such a good reputation, he said he'd looked into my background—to make sure I wasn't a nut. He told me I checked out okay, so he'd go ahead and look for that Scam person—who he'd heard of, by the way—and then he'd find out why Falcon lied about me." She balled her fists in exasperation. "Can you believe it? He checked me out?"

"He probably knows Falcon. Don't take it personally."

"Darn that Hobart, he wasted three perfectly good days," she lamented morosely. "I just want this thing over. I mean, I'm furious with Dean, but I suppose if somebody told me he'd been messing around, my first reaction would be to ... to ..."

"To what?"

She looked over at Nick. He was watching the road, but she had a feeling he was interested in what she was saying. "Oh, strike back, I guess. Maybe yell at him and tell him to get out of my life. But—but then when I cooled down, I'd let him explain. Or at least, I hope I would. Oh, I don't know.... I'm so confused." She sighed. "I guess I can't stand the thought that Dean and I are really through."

He pressed his lips together, but didn't respond. After a moment he gestured to the right. "Look there. You can see it through the trees."

She peered out the car window. "You mean Mrs. Dimm's house?"

"It's more like a castle."

Her depression over her situation faded slightly at the prospect of visiting a real castle. Straining to see, she scanned the tops of the tall autumn-colored trees. For an instant Alice saw a wink of gray—she thought—but the sky was bursting into magenta with the setting of the sun. Against nature's shimmering glory it was hard to distinguish anything so earthbound and mortally inspired as a mere castle.

They rounded another curve in the road, and suddenly a monstrously grotesque building loomed before them. Twisted battlements, towers and chimneys reached up to pierce an already bloody sky. As Alice stared at the silhouette, which canted precariously at the edge of a steep granite bluff, fear knotted her stomach.

She hugged herself and heard Nick's chuckle. "My heavens," she whispered. "It's like something out of a gothic novel. Where's the baying wolf and scary organ music?"

"If you like the castle, you'll love its mistress." He didn't glance at her. Instead, he concentrated on keeping them from plunging into the deep gorge.

Squinting against the brightness of the setting sun, Alice caught sight of several hawks soaring above the sinister jumble of spires. Faced with the frightful actuality of this place, she began to wish she hadn't so quickly agreed to come. "Is—is Mrs. Dimm quite sane?"

"Let's just say she's not dangerous," Nick replied, as he turned the car off the cliffside road and headed onto a lane that was all but invisible in the dense forest and encroaching dusk. Minutes later, they reached an ornately carved archway of native granite, its once-mighty gate rusted ajar. Nick got out and pulled the gate wide, the afflicted joints howling and grinding as though suffering the agonies of torture. Somewhere in the distance, an owl hooted, and Alice nearly screamed with fright.

When Nick climbed back in the car, he gave her a cautious look. "I can see you're starting to regret this."

She realized her mouth was gaping and closed it, managing a grin. "Are you kidding? I love it." That had to be the biggest lie she'd ever told.

Laughing, he inched the car forward over a weed-infested drive paved with irregular slabs of rock. On both sides, the tangle of wildly overgrown rosebushes and shrubs pressed against the car like beseeching hands, filling the air with the screeches of thorns against metal.

"Why does she live this way?" Alice asked over the skin-crawling din. "Can't she afford to keep the place up?"

"Her late husband, Herman Dimm, invented the Dimm orthopedic insole. When a major shoe manufacturer bought his patent in the early seventies, it left him a millionaire. That's when he bought the castle for his bride, Zarta."

"I'd say it's about time she hired a yardman," she said.

"She can't keep help."

"That's right, I forgot," Alice said with a nod. "You told me she was a witch."

"That's one reason. The other is that the place is haunted."

She peered at him as he stopped the car, for one second almost believing his remark. Then her good sense returned, and she grinned. "That's happy news," she teased. "I was wondering where we'd get a fourth for bridge."

"We're here," was his only reply. When he glanced at her, his features were unreadable.

She turned to survey the house, which was illuminated only by the car's headlights. With a rush of new trepidation, she sat forward, trying to see beyond the twin beams of light. The dour gray fortress was a veritable pile of twisted columns, tilted chimneys and Gothic ornamentation.

Directly in front of them, Alice could see wide marble steps that led to a double-doored entry, framed on either side by gargantuan columns shaped like cobras poised to strike.

Before each snake column crouched a sphinx, twice as tall as a man, their weathered, fractured faces exotic and forbidding. The entry to the castle was six feet above their heads, and the doors themselves were at least fifteen feet tall. "Who owned this place before the Dimms? Goliath?" Alice asked in a hushed, shaky voice.

"An old prospector with lots of gold but not much taste."

"Was he sane?"

"By all accounts. But his young wife was rumored to be rather odd."

Alice swallowed and shivered, wondering again what she'd gotten herself into.

Nick switched off the car engine. "Time to go in," he said, getting out of the car. "The lights will stay on for a minute. Let's go."

He was halfway around to help her out, when she flung herself from the car and hurried to the trunk to retrieve her bag. He joined her there. "Don't panic," he said softly. "I didn't bring you here as a human sacrifice."

"I know that," she blurted out, her voice high-pitched and quavering.

He grinned compassionately as he tugged her suitcase from the trunk. "That prospector I told you about—Denby Percival was his name. Anyway, he struck it rich back in the late 1800s and built this place. I guess he figured plain meant poor, so gaudy must mean rich. There was nothing sinister in his motives. It was simply bad taste." He pulled his own suitcase out and indicated that she should precede him to the entrance. "Herman Dimm bought Percival Castle twenty-one years ago, and only lived a year after he bought it, so he and Zarta hadn't done much redecorating. After he died, Zarta lost interest in everything and has left the place as it was."

"She's still grieving twenty years later?" Alice asked, as she started up the stairs. She was amazed at the depth of the woman's bereavement and the thought struck her—would she grieve for Dean as long?

When Nick didn't reply, she turned and saw that he'd remained at the bottom of the steps. His expression was obscured in shadow, but Alice had a feeling his thoughts were bleak. "Nick?" she coaxed. "You okay?"

He snapped his head up at the sound of her voice, and she knew he'd returned from wherever he'd gone. Nodding, he loped up the steps until he was beside her. Just then, the car headlights went out.

A slice of fear cut through her. She didn't like the dark. Never had. She knew her fear was a silly remnant of her childhood and worked to shake it off. "The scenery's beautiful here," she managed faintly. "If you're a bat."

"Take my arm," Nick said, sounding comfortingly nearby. "Some of the steps are broken."

"For once I wish I smoked. We could light a match." She groped in the dark and touched his buttock. With an embarrassed intake of breath, she drew her hand away. "Oh. Sorry."

He chuckled. "From that clue you ought to be able to find my arm."

"I'll keep that in mind," she said, attempting to sound unruffled.

She was thankful for the cover of darkness; her blush would have been incriminating. She hadn't expected to touch him so intimately, but now that she had, the experience stayed with her. With great care, she moved her hand down until she came in contact with the suitcase he was holding. Then she ran her fingers forward until she grazed his fist on the handle. Raising her hand a few inches, she found his wrist and grasped it.

"Can you see well enough to start up the steps?" he asked.

"Fine. Uh, just fine . . ."

He moved forward with her in tow. After she counted eight more steps, they reached the flat expanse before the doors. Nick set down the cases, and she let go of his wrist. Her eyes had become accustomed enough to see him reach for a knocker that was as big as a basketball. She could just make it out—another sphinx.

Nick pounded. The metallic sound echoed loudly in the surrounding darkness.

She willed herself to be calm. "Is there somebody in there who can hear? If Zarta Dimm is deaf, we could set off a ton of TNT and it wouldn't rouse her."

"She keeps a skeleton staff, but—"

"Exactly how many skeletons *does* she keep?"

He glanced at her, and she could just detect his grin. "It varies. As I started to say, this knocker's hooked up to flash some lights inside. Even if she were alone, she'd be aware that we were here."

"Oh . . . good." To be honest, she wasn't sure how good she really thought it was. Maybe life as a homeless person wasn't all that bad compared to this.

For a long time nothing happened. Alice was grateful she didn't hear the snarling of wolves or the flap of bat's wings. "Maybe she's out sucking somebody's blood," she said, more to hear the sound of a human voice than because she meant it.

"Zarta doesn't leave the castle."

"Oh, that makes me feel much better," she muttered.

Nick chuckled. "I'm glad to see you're keeping your sense of humor. You'll need it."

After what seemed like another eternity, Nick knocked again, causing the metallic explosions that did Alice's burgeoning headache no good.

"Maybe she's asleep," she whispered. "Are you sure she knows we're coming?"

An ear-piercing shriek split the air, and a scream formed in Alice's throat, but before it could escape, she controlled it, realizing that what she'd heard had been only the creaking of unoiled hinges. One of the huge doors had cracked open, suddenly releasing a shaft of light.

"She knows we're here," Nick said under his breath as a black-shrouded form appeared before them.

She nodded, grateful Nick hadn't noticed her momentary hysteria. Taking a deep breath, like someone about to plunge into an icy river, Alice tried to ready herself. She needed a job. She could handle this.

It took several seconds for her eyes to adjust to the brightness. When they did, she could see pinpoints of light within the shroud and realized it was no shroud at all, but a delicate shawl made of black lace, half concealing the face of a tiny woman.

She appeared to be in her late fifties and was peering at them through the gauzy material. The lace masked her eyes, but not her expression, which was both prim and inhospitable.

Though a three-tiered brass chandelier glittered high above them, the castle had a dingy, cloistered feel. The air itself carried a dankness that made Alice's heart race with long-suppressed memories of her dismal childhood. She was appalled by the jumble of emotions the place fomented in her mind, causing an irrational cowardice that was difficult to quell.

Before she could gather her wits enough to introduce herself, she saw that Mrs. Dimm's attention was fixed on Nick. Alice turned, too, startled to see him raise his hands to sign a greeting.

With brusque movements Mrs. Dimm signed back, "You're late. Dinner is cold. Get the woman settled in the Lavender Room. I'll be in the dining salon." Dismissively, she swirled away, her floor-length shawl billowing behind her as she moved along a hallway dark with rich wood panels and hanging Flemish tapestries.

Alice could only stare after the petite, yet commanding dowager until she disappeared around a corner. Letting out a long-held breath, she turned her gaze to the man beside her. "You—you sign?"

He shoved his hands into his pockets as though he'd committed some offense with them. "Didn't I tell you?" he asked, but Alice had a feeling he knew full well he hadn't.

"I think there's a lot you haven't told me about yourself," she said, a trace of censure in her voice, though she wasn't truly angry. Signing was no crime. More like a delightful surprise. She was just sorry he hadn't shared his talent with her. She wondered what else he'd decided not to share. "So, how is it you know how to sign for the deaf?"

He picked up her bag in one hand and clutched her fingers in the other. "Let's get you settled. Zarta's waiting dinner for us."

He hustled her through the huge octagonal foyer to a staircase that swept grandly upward, dividing partway into two beneath a wood-paneled wall covered with stern-faced portraits. Alice grabbed at the ornate banister, steadying herself as Nick rushed her up the steps, then guided her to the left. "The Lavender Room's this way," he directed.

"I figured," she puffed as he dragged her along. "I gather you know the place well?"

"Zarta was my teacher years ago. We kept in touch after she married. I've been here several times."

"And she loves you like a servant?" she asked breathlessly.

"She's a troubled woman, Alice. Her hurt blinds her to a lot." They reached the dimly lit second floor, where more dark paneled walls were covered with more aging, worn tapestries. Nick smiled without humor. "I have a feeling you know the wounded type."

She was startled by his remark. Of course, she did. Her father, for one—poor, bitter soul. "What makes you say that?" she asked, feeling uncomfortable. Could Nick really read minds?

With a small nod of his head he indicated the door behind her. "That's your room. I'm next door—Vincent Price is across the hall."

He started toward the steps, but she halted him with a tug on his wrist. "That's very funny, but don't change the subject. What made you say that about my knowing wounded types?" she demanded, a little irked by his continued evasions.

He shrugged. "You work with deaf kids, don't you?"

She suspected he was hedging but she couldn't figure why. Some deaf kids were certainly wounded little souls. The world wasn't particularly fair to people who were "different." "I suppose so," she finally agreed.

"Zarta's waiting," he reminded. When he reached the stairs, he paused. "Don't bother to change. As soon as she eats, she'll go to bed. Then you'll have time to settle in."

Alice nodded. "I'll just wash up."

He grinned. Oddly, the flash of teeth made her feel fluttery inside. "In that case," he said, "the bath's down the hall. There's no lock, so I'll try to remember to knock."

"Try hard," she joked, smiling and putting aside any nagging doubts she had about him. She liked Nick Street, and she knew in her heart that his intentions were absolutely honorable.

AT THE BOTTOM OF THE stairs Nick immediately turned right and headed for the dining salon. He needed to talk privately with Zarta. When he reached the door, he stumbled to a halt. Everything was as he remembered it from his last visit—with Brenda, his wife. A cannonball of pain slammed his gut and waves of grayness passed over him with the memory. He'd had no idea it would be this painful to come back—alone. Not until he'd driven up to that damned, rusting gate.

He hadn't planned on ever coming back. But that would have been cruel. After all, Zarta was the one person in the world he really owed.

He saw movement at the far end of a room that had once been grand, but was now as desolate as his memories. The rose paneled walls were spotted from years of dampness, and the once-bright gilded cornices were flaking and dull. The massive silver chandelier was black with tarnish, a few of its dusty globes still managing to light the room.

Sitting at a sturdy medieval table, a cracked mirror behind her, was the tiny unsmiling mistress of the castle, the image of a petulant, pampered child. But Nick knew different. He knew the great loss she'd suffered.

He'd known Zarta when she'd been a gentle, loving teacher of deaf children. It was the depth of her caring that had helped him ultimately regain his hearing. He owed her more than he could hope to repay. As he looked at her now, he recalled how lovely and happy she'd been when she became Herman Dimm's young bride over twenty years ago.

Years after Herman's death, she'd bitterly confided to Nick that she'd never thought she could find a man who would take her because she was "damaged goods." But Herman had never seen her deafness as anything other than a part of her specialness.

Then he'd been taken from her—suddenly and ruthlessly. An aneurysm. One blinding flash of pain. He'd grabbed her hand, and when she turned, he managed to feebly sign, "I love you," before he collapsed and died.

With her great love gone, she'd grown sour, hating the world and entombing herself here to endure a living death. She'd admitted she was too cowardly to take her own life, so she awaited death, all the while despising everyone and everything.

Nick supposed he and Zarta weren't much different. Only Nick didn't hate the world; he just hated himself. He could have—should have—done something to save the people he loved most in the world. But he hadn't, and that was his hell. He'd have to live with his failure. Because he'd failed the ones he'd loved, he tried to atone every day by helping people through his work. He couldn't be a cop anymore because of the nerve and muscle damage to his right arm, but he could help—he *did* help, damn it. Why the hell else would he be here with Alice?

He heard a whacking sound and realized Zarta had slammed her palm on the table to get his attention. As soon as he looked up, she began to sign, "Are you blind as well as muddleheaded, Dominic? Answer me!"

He walked to her and kissed her cool, pale cheek, signing, "Remember, I'm Nick Street for now. We'll have to change my sign name."

She gave him a disgusted look. "I don't care what name you go by as long as you brought me an assistant. I just hope you haven't lost what little sense you have!"

"I love you, too, sweetheart." He grinned, then touched her shoulder affectionately. "And thank you for letting me impose on you this way."

She shrugged. "I need an assistant, Dominic. Besides that, you can do some of the heavy lifting Jetter can't handle."

He flexed his injury-weakened right arm. "Well, I can try, anyway." Then, switching back to the subject that had brought him in here, he reminded, "Don't sign a *D* at your lips, sweetheart," he reminded, referring to the way his sign name was made. "I've been thinking about it. What about signing an *N* by your mouth? Tell her it's because I have a great smile."

She frowned. "I thought that was how you got that sign name."

He shook his head. "No, the smile came later—when I met you." He touched her cheek fondly, but as usual, she backed away, so he went on, pretending not to notice her huffy withdrawal. "My first teacher gave that sign name to me because I tried to mouth words like my folks did."

"I'm an old woman. How can I remember a new sign name after all these years? Such foolishness!"

"You're as sharp as ever, you old fraud. Promise me. It's important. Now show me—an *N* beside your mouth."

She continued to pout, but made the new sign name, shorthand for a person's whole name, traditionally bestowed on someone by a deaf friend.

"That's wonderful, Zarta." He made her sign name, a "Zorro" swish in the air across his chin, then decided it was time to change the subject. He had no idea when Alice might walk in. "And how is Jetter doing these days?"

She eyed heaven. "He's so crippled up he's more dangerous than useful. The whole staff is as lazy as bedbugs!"

Nick shook his head at her. "So nothing's changed." He glanced at the table, set with a jumble of mismatched china and silver. In the center of it all was a big sliver tureen. "Smells good."

"Potato soup, but it's cold."

"Vichyssoise," he signed. "I love it."

She slapped at his hands testily. "You're a fool, Dominic!"

Distressed that she was continuing to use that damning name, he took both her hands in his and knelt beside her, staring solemnly into her veiled eyes. "It's *N* beside your lips, not *D*," he mouthed slowly.

With a guttural cry, she yanked free. "You know I could never lip-read! You're a mean and cruel boy to taunt me that way!"

He'd forgotten she was so sensitive about her inability to read lips. In the deaf community lipreading was considered a gift rather than a skill. "I'm sorry, Zarta. But, remember to use my new sign name while Alice is here."

She pounded the table with her small, blue-veined hand. "You try my patience to the breaking point! Why must you insist on playing foolish games?"

He detected movement out of the corner of his eye and turned to see Alice standing in the doorway, staring curiously at them.

He flinched, hoping Zarta's last sign hadn't slung all his efforts at the fan!

4

NICK'S LUCK HELD THAT first night. Alice must not have been at the door for more than a few seconds. Fortunately, thanks to the housekeeper's haphazard way of table setting, a spoon had dropped to the floor, and Nick managed to come up with it in his hand, masking the real reason he'd been down on one knee.

The most pleasant thing he discovered that night was Alice's sign name—an *A* and *W* over her heart, which also signaled that someone in the deaf community thought she was a loving person. He was far from surprised by that. What did surprise him was that Zarta remembered his new sign name.

For the next three days Nick silently witnessed Alice going about her duties, cheerfully helping Zarta as combination companion/secretary—a taxing job, if for no other reason than that Zarta managed to find fault with every single thing she did. He heard the familiar thwack of Zarta's hand slamming wood and knew Alice was being admonished for another imagined infraction.

His fists tightened on the railing that prevented him from plunging to the floor of the misty valley far below the castle. But even though he was outside on the first-floor portico, he was not out of earshot. One of the tall, mullioned doors to the drawing room stood ajar. Heavy velvet curtains were drawn shut, allowing him to go unseen by either his hostess or her new companion.

He heard the rustle of fabric, which told him that someone had come out onto the windswept patio. Turning, he saw Alice standing there in classy houndstooth slacks, a matching blazer and white blouse. Her quick smile sent an unexpected rush of pleasure through him, and he found himself smiling back. "Hi," he said. "How's it going?"

"No worse than having a room full of cranky kindergartners on a rainy day." She pushed back a strand of hair that the wind had blown across her eyes. "Did you know Zarta plans to write her husband's biography? Apparently Herman was quite an exceptional man. He invented more than that insole."

"Yes, I know."

She lifted her chin in pretended smugness. "Well, did you also know that I'm the lucky one that gets to go through all his old papers and arrange them in chronological order?"

"Don't let it go to your head," he said wryly.

She laughed. "Zarta also told me the assistant she's advertising for must have publishing credentials so he or she can help write Herman's story."

"It's a book that probably should be written. Herman Dimm was actually very bright—if you'll pardon the pun. And it's a shame he died so young. I'm glad she's starting to work on the book."

"Zarta said she's had trouble getting the project going, since her assistants keep quitting."

Clearly Zarta hadn't told Alice why they kept quitting—fear of the resident ghost, Theora Percival. Nick decided not to bring it up, either. Maybe Theora wouldn't appear while Alice was here.

"To be honest," she admitted, "I'm not crazy about rummaging around in dark, musty places looking for Herman's notes and documents. Basements give me the creeps, but I—I know that's childish. I promised Zarta that first thing tomorrow I'd start dragging stuff out of the storage rooms." She looked at him sheepishly. "You might get to help with the heavier stuff—if you beg."

When she gave him a wistful smile, he discovered with some shock that his interest in her had grown beyond the simple desire to help someone in need. Her shiny black hair beckoned to be touched, and her soft jacket tantalized him with promises of ripe, hidden curves. Her full lips gleamed in subtle invitation. He found himself craving her with an intensity, a hunger, that unnerved him. "I'm not going anywhere," he said, his voice vaguely hoarse.

She moved up beside him and peered over the rail. "Jeez! A bungee jumper's paradise—but I think I'll pass." She backed away, rubbing her arms with her hands. "It's nippy out here. Aren't you cold?"

He was wearing wool flannel slacks and an oversize crewneck sweater so the gun at his back would be hidden. It was hard to find casual clothes that concealed the .38, but he knew the consequences of leaving it behind. "I'm very warm-blooded," he said, nodding toward the drawing room where Zarta sat in her perpetual darkness. "Is she driving you nuts?"

The sound she made was half laugh, half sigh. "For such a little woman, she has one big dorsal fin."

"She can be quite the shark," he agreed.

"She told me to get out and leave her alone. Said I was raising too much dust with my endless fussing."

"I have to give you credit," he said. "You're holding up very well. I don't see murder in your eyes, yet."

"Zarta's not the first difficult person I've had to deal with." As she leaned back against the rough granite wall beside the railing, Nick noticed shadows beneath her eyes. She was exhausted, and it troubled him.

Alice laughed at some internal thought, but it was a wan, weary sound. "Despite Zarta's blustering and face-making and slamming of tables, I think she likes me." She tipped her head back. "We'll get along just fine. You'll see."

He frowned down at her. "Have you been sleeping okay?"

Her smile faded. "Uh, sure."

He sensed the lie and moved to lounge against the wall. Her light perfume filled his nostrils. He tried to resist its warming effect but couldn't seem to force his mind to other things. "Why aren't you sleeping?" he asked, inching nearer, though he knew he shouldn't.

She looked away and shook her head. He watched her lips—those compelling, sexy lips—as she spoke. "Oh, Nick . . . I feel so alone." Shifting, she faced him.

"I'm thankful Zarta's keeping me busy. It helps take my mind off—off everything. But the nights, the nights are—"

She halted, gulping to steady her voice. Tears formed and quivered on her lower lashes, giving Nick a glimpse of the unhappiness she'd been hiding. Like an arrow, her sadness found its target in some vulnerable and unguarded place within him, and he winced at the painful stab of sympathy her admission caused.

For the past five years he'd been a man who was never really happy or unhappy. He'd been conscious only of a numbing hollowness, and he'd been content to live with that.

Damn it, he didn't want to care. When he started to move away, she took his hand. "I know things weren't perfect between Dean and me, Nick." She blinked and a tear stole slowly down her cheek. "I mean, he was possessive, even domineering, I suppose. But how could he love me unconditionally one day and despise me the next? I—I just don't understand that. I feel as if I've been pushed off a cliff."

He hesitated, his gaze drawn to her sad eyes. Angry that she'd made him feel this way, he had to fight back the urge to retort bitterly, "Maybe Silvanus's hands were so dirty he wanted a clean towel to wipe them on." That was his personal theory—that her goodness and kindness had attracted Silvanus. He wouldn't be surprised if Silvanus had imagined he would become good and decent if he married such a person. And now that he believed his perfect little Alice was corrupt, Silvanus had felt swindled. Nick knew it would be cruel to suggest such a thing to Alice, though. She had no idea her ex-fiancé was suspected of any wrongdoing.

With an angry flexing of his jaw, he blocked a morose chuckle. What the hell did he know about it, anyway? He was no psychologist. For all he knew, Silvanus was a normal guy who'd thought he'd been two-timed and had become rightfully angry. He looked down at her delicate face and didn't know what to say. The truth was out of the question. He wanted badly to leave, but the gentle tug of her fingers on his held him as surely as a heavy chain.

"Nick?" she whispered, squeezing his hand. Her expression was questioning and apprehensive.

"Yes?" As he searched her face—those glimmering eyes and that seductive, full mouth—his body ached with a fierce hunger. He wanted to feel those lips beneath his, yielding and urgent with passion.

"Have you ever just hugged a woman?" she asked, so softly he wasn't sure he'd even heard her right.

"Done what?"

"Hugged a woman? Just to comfort her?"

Painful visions of his wife rushed through his mind. He gritted his teeth, forcing the memories back.

"Nick . . . I—I really need a hug."

That innocent plea sent a rush of feeling through him that was impossible to ignore. For days she'd filled his senses to dangerous levels with her sexy scent and her gentle, nurturing manner. He fought to control his growing desire and felt the erotic stroking of her breeze-tossed hair against his cheek. He was surprised at how close he was to her now. When had he moved?

"I—I'm sorry, Nick," she murmured. Apparently his expression made it evident he wasn't happy about her request, for she began to toy nervously with her lower lip. "I always told my students just to let me know if they needed a hug. I didn't think—"

His mouth claimed hers suddenly, passionately, surprising both of them. He felt a breathless wonder in the first heady touch of those lips, but in his heart he knew only resentment. Why were his emotions betraying him so thoroughly with this woman? She'd wanted a simple little hug—between friends—and he'd wanted nothing at all. So what the hell was he doing kissing her?

He heard a strangled cry deep in her throat. No doubt she was horrified and disgusted by this display—any second now, her knee would slam into his groin.

But the knee didn't come. Instead, she nestled against him, her hands slowly slipping from his chest to his back, and her lips opening slightly, then more and more. His tongue met the smooth wetness of her teeth, and he felt a wild surge of pleasure as her tongue languidly entwined with his.

He felt her yield as he pressed her tightly to him, all the while acquainting himself with the dark, silky recesses of her mouth. The experience was wonderfully seductive and more stirring than he'd ever imagined it could be. She moaned, but this time it was the unmistakable sound of surrender. She clung to him, and he

felt her tremble as her fingers began to massage, to ex-
plore—

Good God! His gun! *You're an idiot, Falcon!* he riled
inwardly, wrenching away from her with an obscenity
on his lips.

"Hell," he muttered, his voice gruff. "I'm sorry."
Somehow, he felt stiff and sore and battered. Running
a fist across his lip, he checked for blood. He stared at
his hand, surprised to see it was shaking. There was, of
course, no blood, but his fingers were still heated by her
warmth. Knowing he was a complete fool for kissing
her, he ran his fingers roughly through his hair to rid
himself of the feel of her. He was rattled, and he wasn't
used to that.

Looking down, he saw Alice was flushed, her eyes
wide and glassy as she sagged against the granite wall.

Angry and disgusted with himself, he pivoted away.
"I'm not a saint, Alice, and I don't hug."

ALICE'S ROOM WAS DARK, decorated in strong shades of
lavender and purple. The walls were covered with faded
lavender fabric, and garlands of nuts and leaves were
carved into the yellowed ceiling. Portraits of purple
landscapes, mauve bouquets and violet-clad children
covered the walls, all encased in timeworn, gilded
frames.

The arched floor-to-ceiling French doors were shuttered and curtainless, making the room seem dead and
forbidding. The first morning she'd awakened in that
room she'd flung open the shutters, allowing sunshine

inside—the only sun the room had seen in decades, she was sure.

Across from the four-poster bed was a dainty lavender sofa that ladies of ages past had probably lounged upon to recover from fainting spells. Between the two thick-walled French doors that led out onto a tiny balcony, was a small writing desk, and beside the bed stood a Queen Anne chest-on-chest. All the furniture was walnut, and to Alice's great relief, free of mildew or rot.

It was late, after ten, and she was drained both physically and emotionally. With a heavy sigh, she lay back on her squeaky four-poster and stared up at the bluish-purple canopy that hovered like a storm cloud above her head.

Nick had kissed her today. It had been hours and hours ago, but the memory was no less vivid now than it had been when he'd pulled her into his arms.

The whole thing had been like a crazy dream. At first she'd been so stunned she hadn't known what to do. Then, in the blink of an eye, she hadn't cared about anything but his electrifying lips! In a matter of seconds she'd gone completely, unequivocally crazy, because she'd kissed him back.

She closed her eyes, then opened them when all she could conjure was his rugged, gorgeous face and those haunting, tormented eyes. Her pulse rate shot up to double its normal speed just picturing him in her mind. What was the matter with her? If any other man had kissed her that way, she'd have slapped his arrogant face and told him off. But with Nick, she'd only stared, feeling weak—and wonderful. She had to admit, if only to herself, that she'd thought he was terribly attractive from the moment she'd found herself straddling him on the sidewalk after he'd saved her life. But she'd put the idea from her mind. After all, she'd been engaged.

She drew herself up into a protective little ball. Lord, she was tired. And sad and lonely and confused and— and turned-on! She didn't want to be any of those things. She just wanted to be Mrs. Dean Silvanus, damn it! With another sigh, she covered her face with her hands. "Why did you kiss me, Nick?" she mumbled. "Why did I kiss you back?"

A little voice inside her was pestering her about something, but she refused to listen. It was suggesting something about her seeking him out, leading him on. But that wasn't true at all. She liked Nick as a friend. He'd been kind to her when what she'd needed desperately was kindness. She'd simply wanted a hug.

A hug! the little voice argued. *You're wounded and you're angry with Dean and you're human. You want to feel—wanted. You tempted him into kissing you, and he did. So quit whining and get on with your life.* She bolted upright, horrified. Had she really been so unconsciously manipulative? She shook her head, hoping that it wasn't true.

Nick had certainly made himself scarce for the rest of the day. He hadn't even come to dinner. She'd seen him once, walking around in the weed-infested garden near a stone gazebo. He'd looked angry. It was perfectly plain he'd only been trying to help her when he'd brought her here. Oh, she had a feeling they'd both felt some mutual attraction, but she also sensed he didn't want it to go any further than that.

Well, she'd certainly make sure it didn't go any further! He was a private man with no desire to get involved, and she was a woman trying to get her ex-fiancé back. There was no reason to act on any attraction—they were adults, after all.

Rising, she hurriedly undressed and slipped on a terry robe, deciding a hot bath would soothe her raw nerves. She went to the chest-on-chest to get her nightgown. Opening the bottom drawer, she was startled to see a man's wristwatch lying among her lingerie. Perplexed, she lifted the watch, already sure whose it was—she'd seen it on Nick's wrist. Turning it, she checked the back where she found an inscription that read: Nick—I'll Love You Forever. Brenda.

Brenda? Alice peered at the name, wondering about the woman who'd given Nick this watch. Who was she? Where was she? But then other, more immediate questions struck her. What was Nick's watch doing in her drawer? What had he been looking for?

First Dean, then Dominic Falcon, then Mort Hobart had callously invaded her privacy. And now *Nick?* This was too much! How *dare* he! How dare *any* of them!

She jerked around to glare at the bedroom door, trying to decide what to do. She only hoped he'd have a good explanation. Not about Brenda—that wasn't any of her business—but for why his watch was in her drawer.

Clutching the watch, she marched along the dark, shadowy hallway to Nick's room and knocked. She flinched at the loudness of her angry raps in the oppressive stillness. For a moment she heard nothing. Then there was a soft thud as though Nick had lowered his feet to the floor. Apparently he'd gone to bed.

"Just a second," he called softly.

She stiffened, parting her lips to utter a scathing response, but for some reason she couldn't make a sound.

The door opened as Nick cinched the sash of a navy terry robe. A flicker of surprise crossed his face before his features closed in a wary frown. "If you're here for your apology, then—I'm sorry about the kiss." He plunged his hands into his robe pockets, his stare somber and unnerving.

She started to upbraid him, but found herself staring at a bit more chest than she'd been prepared for, and she had to make quick work of squelching a feminine quiver of appreciation. "Uh, you—you've already apologized for that," she stammered, dropping her glance to his waist, which was an equally unsettling sight. What was the matter with her? She'd come over to yell at him for going through her things, and instead, she was stuttering like a nervous beginner in a public-speaking class. "Anyway..." she confessed in a whisper, "I'm not sure the kiss was totally your fault."

He was quiet, and she felt compelled to check his expression. Lifting a worried gaze, she discovered that he was studying her intently. "Is that why you came?" he asked. "To admit that?"

She shook her head, trying to remind herself that she was furious with this man. "No, I came—"

"I'm not going to kiss you again, Alice."

She was shocked by his blunt remark. It sounded like a warning, as if he thought she wanted him to kiss her again; as if she'd come over here to *ask* for it! Her cheeks grew fiery with indignation and just a shade of guilt, since she really wouldn't have minded a second kiss. "Is that what you think I want? To have you kiss me again?" she hissed, unsettled by both his audacity and his embarrassing insight. "Why—why that's the most egotistical thing I've ever heard!"

Angrier than she'd ever been in her life, she threw his watch at him. Amazingly, he caught it before it struck him—which made her even angrier. "I came over here to tell you I found your watch—or should I call it 'incriminating evidence'!" she accused, spinning away. "Obviously you're no better than Dean *or* Falcon!"

PUTTING ASIDE HIS BOOK, Nick shoved himself up from a worn leather chair by a crackling fire and walked out onto the drawing-room portico to get some fresh air. He took a deep breath, but it didn't ease his restlessness. Colorful leaves twirled and danced around him in delirious abandon. A few dropped out of the sky, splashing vivid color into the gray corners of the veranda.

They reminded him of Alice—a vivid bit of color that had fallen unbidden into his gray life. He stared out over the cliff face. In the distance, mountains were haloed by the golden-pink rays of the setting sun—another bit of beauty that assailed his senses.

Glancing at his watch, he remembered how angry Alice had been when she'd pitched it at his face. Twisting away from the fiery sunset, he ground out a curse.

It was nearly dinnertime, and he'd hardly seen Alice all day. She'd been avoiding him. He'd have to be as insensitive as a rock not to have noticed it. It was better this way, he decided. Even though she'd started removing boxes of Herman's things from the dank basement she disliked so much, she'd coolly rejected his offer of help. He closed his eyes against the memory of the frostiness that crept into her manner whenever she saw him coming. In her expressive eyes he could see regret, distrust and anger. He could tell she didn't hate him. She probably didn't have hate in her. But she didn't like, and didn't understand, what she perceived he'd done.

Restless and irritated, he turned back to squint at the last bright gasps of the dying day. The damned thing with the watch was probably just as well. She might as well believe he was a lying weasel. That was an easier explanation to swallow than the other one—the real one. He could just see himself trying to tell her. "Hey, Alice, it wasn't me, it was Theora, the resident ghost." On the credibility scale, that ranked right up there with, "The check is in the mail."

He'd hoped Theora would remain inactive during Alice's stay. Months could go by without a single sign that she was around. Irritation clenching his belly, he gave the castle a stern perusal and muttered to the air, "Very ironic, Theora. But in your own demented way, you did me a favor."

He didn't relish the idea that every time Alice looked at him she was regretting ever putting her trust in him. But, on the plus side, if she kept her distance, then he wouldn't have to worry about losing control again.

Some small, faraway sound drew his attention and he frowned, puzzled. Could it really be a car engine? People so rarely came here.

Apprehension scurried along his spine like a spider. Spinning around, he stalked through the dusky drawing room, then hurried down the hall to the staircase. Taking the steps two at a time, he got to the second floor quickly. Knowing the rooms that faced the drive were never locked, he slipped inside the first one, its mustiness hitting him like a moldy dustrag as he crossed to throw open a shuttered window. Just as he did, a black sedan pulled to a halt before the door and a man got out. He was husky and wore an expensive-looking suit. Nick had seen him before—with Silvanus. Evangeline. That was his name. A bodyguard or leg breaker—probably both.

He was glad he'd moved his car to the other side of the castle. He didn't want Evangeline wondering what a car with a Missouri license plate was doing here.

He heard the door knocker thud loudly, its echo resounding along the empty corridors. Since this was a seldom-used room, he wasn't surprised that no lights had been rigged to flash.

Curious about why Silvanus's flunky was here, he moved silently into the hall and flattened himself against the wall nearest the stairway so that he could hear whatever explanation Evangeline gave.

Faltering steps grew louder and louder along the hallway. Nick recognized the sound of Jetter, the old caretaker. Not long after the footfalls stopped, the door hinges shrieked.

"Yes, sir?" Jetter croaked politely.

"I want to see Alice Woods," came the flat voice of Silvanus's man.

"Won't you come in?"

The door wailed and then thudded shut. "Would you care to go to the drawing room, sir?"

"I'll wait here."

"Yes, sir."

"Just a minute," Evangeline said. "Who's here besides Miss Woods?"

"Excuse me, sir?"

"I said, who's here besides Miss Woods?" he shouted, clearly thinking the old man was hard of hearing.

Nick stiffened. Jetter had known him for years—as Dominic Falcon. Even though he'd told the old man to call him "Nick" during this visit, Jetter was a bit absentminded, so he wasn't sure it had registered.

"Well, now, sir—"

"What is this?" demanded a feminine voice—Alice's. Her clipped footfalls were rapidly approaching. "What are you doing here, Mr. Evangeline?" There was a pause of a few beats. "Is Dean all right? Did he send you?"

"Yeah, he sent me." He chuckled. "You're good. You sound like you give a damn."

There was another pause, longer this time, and Nick was sure that Alice and the bodyguard were communicating a great deal with their eyes.

"My Lord," she gasped after a minute. "You're checking on me!"

Evangeline said nothing. Apparently, he wasn't planning to deny her accusation.

"Dean has some nerve!" she cried. "He's the one who dumped *me*. Doesn't he know I'm not his property?"

There was a croaky cough. It sounded like the old caretaker was uncomfortable but helpless to intercede. Nick didn't blame him. Evangeline was an intimidating thug.

"You can go, Jetter," Alice said kindly. "I can handle this."

The old man's shuffling footsteps were hesitant at first, but gradually grew fainter and fainter until they disappeared.

"How did you find me?" Alice asked, sounding as though she was trying to regain her composure.

"You left this address with your landlord. He said you left with some suit."

Nick's stomach clenched, and he held his breath.

"A friend of Mrs. Dimm's brought me here since it's so hard to find," she said. When she revealed nothing more, Nick blessed her. "What exactly does Dean think I'm doing? Having an orgy with my lover, Scam, and all his felonious friends?"

"It's not my job to know what the boss is thinking. My job is just to check on you."

"Well, that's quite a noble job," she mocked. "Look. Dean dropped me. I'd quit teaching—at his insistence—and therefore had little money. I'm sure he's already aware of that. I'm here because I heard about a woman who needed a paid companion for a while. Not that it's any of Dean's business. That's the only explanation I'm giving you. Now I want you to go."

"Let me see the lady."

"She's eating her dinner."

"Are you afraid to let me see her?"

Nick heard a noise he couldn't quite recognize. A scuffling sound.

"Don't push me, sweetheart," Evangeline retorted insolently. "I've got a job to do."

Nick stiffened, automatically reaching for his gun. He steeled himself, listening intently. Alice was still laboring under the assumption that her ex-fiancé was merely a businessman. She wouldn't be prepared for just how lethal this flunky could become.

Nick decided if there was even the slightest sound of a struggle or even if the silence grew overlong, he would blow his cover, blow everything, to save Alice from being harmed by that piece of garbage.

"Get out of here!" she cried, her voice tremulous and offended. "And tell Dean if he wants to talk to me, I'll do it face-to-face or not at all."

"You know, I almost believe you're really taking care of some old woman. By the way," he drawled. "Did you know that Falcon's disappeared?"

"Good riddance," she said. "Now, why don't you do the same?"

"They told me in town that a crazy old lady lived up here with a ghost. I thought it was a load of crap, but now that I see this spook house, I guess that's what I'll tell Mr. Silvanus. Maybe you aren't screwing around, after all."

Nick heard the door squeal and realized it was being yanked open.

"Get out!" Alice screamed.

A low chuckle reached Nick, a filthy little sound, and it made Nick's aversion for the man mushroom into a living, breathing hatred. It was all he could do to keep from bolting down the stairs and slamming the scumbag in his fat, sneering face.

He heard the scrape of a shoe, then footsteps, and realized Evangeline was leaving.

The slam of the door was deafening, echoing for a full minute through the huge house.

Nick eased away from the wall and peered around the corner. Alice stood facing the door. She was very still and her hands were cupped over her mouth as though she was trying to hold back a sob.

He wanted to take her in his arms, comfort her—make love to her. Damn. Having kissed her, it was hard for him to turn his back on her despair and do nothing. He was sure that was what was driving Silvanus, too. It was obvious he wasn't over her, despite Nick's falsified report.

"This complicates matters," he muttered. If Silvanus was anything, he was a man who got what he wanted. And it looked as if he still wanted Alice.

Nick's attention was drawn by movement from below. Alice was walking toward the dining salon, her pumps beating out a slow, even tat-a-tat on the marble floor. He watched her go, admiring her strength of character. She'd composed herself, squared her shoulders and was moving with absolute control. She wouldn't let Zarta see that she was upset. Just as she wouldn't let him see. She no longer considered him her confidant or friend.

Feeling a renewed sense of yearning, he mouthed a curse. He didn't want to see her again—ever in his life—but more than that, he didn't want to see her hurt.

"Luke," he growled under his breath, "you'd better hurry and build your blasted case!"

5

THE CASTLE WAS SILENT, almost tomblike, but Alice couldn't sleep. She just lay in bed, gazing aimlessly about. The dreariness of her bedroom was less detectable in the silvery wash of moonglow. The only sound was the occasional howl of the wind leaching its way through crevices.

The room felt stuffy, but she didn't want to open a window. Her balcony overlooked the terrifying drop to the valley floor, and being jittery about heights, she had trouble enough walking near the closed French doors. She would rather face a loaded gun than unlock the barrier that separated her from the empty void below.

She shivered at the idea and turned away from the moonlit windows, squeezing her eyes shut and trying not to think. It had to be after two in the morning, and she needed to be up by six. Unfortunately, thoughts of Mr. Evangeline's surprise visit churned in her mind. It was clear that Dean was having second thoughts about dumping her so heartlessly. And now she tossed and turned, bedeviled by a parade of conflicting emotions. She'd been in love with Dean, and happy that such an important man loved her—but then he'd treated her so badly.

She'd just about come to the conclusion that Dean would have to do some pretty fancy groveling to get her back, but that in the end, she might forgive him. She had as much pride as he had nerve. But she couldn't help being impressed that ultimately he was inclined to trust her, despite the damning report Dominic Falcon had turned in.

It surprised her to learn that the private investigator was missing. No doubt he was hiding, aware that his lie was about to be found out. Whatever else happened, whether she reconciled with Dean or not, she was determined to prove her innocence and get Dominic Falcon's license revoked. No man that incompetent should ever be allowed to work as a private investigator.

She heard a sound and tensed. It wasn't the wind, but rather a barely audible creaking. Alice recognized it as the noise the hall floor made when someone stepped on an uneven board. She'd only heard it when Nick was either coming or going from his room. Opening her eyes, she focused on her door, not sure why. The moonlight fell across the doorknob, making it clearly visible.

She wasn't really surprised when she saw the cut-crystal knob twinkle in the moonlight as it turned. But no one knocked on the door to rouse her. In fact, the only sound was the barely audible squeak the hinges made as the door swung inward. Had she been asleep, she would have heard nothing.

Swallowing hard, she stared, frozen. She'd already warned Nick once about invading her privacy, and she couldn't believe he'd have the gall to do it again—especially in the middle of the night when he had to know she was here. She didn't think his intentions were violent, but she had no idea why she felt so sure about that. She held her breath, trying to decide what to do. Should she pretend to sleep and watch to see what he did? Should she jump up and confront him? She vacillated nervously, gazing at the open door, wondering, waiting.

He didn't come in. He didn't even get far enough into the doorway for her to see him. The bedroom door just stood ajar, proof only that she hadn't been dreaming the whole thing. Her adrenaline level shot up and her pulse began to throb in her temples. Somehow Nick's failure to materialize was more threatening than if he'd walked in and started rifling through her purse.

Then she heard the creaking sound again—as though that uneven piece of board in the hallway was being trod on. She would have expected to hear his footsteps, too.

What kind of game was Nick playing? Before she fully realized what she was doing, she hopped out of bed and grabbed her robe. Tying the sash, she tiptoed to her doorway. She peered into the hall, looking first toward the staircase, then in the direction of Nick's room. She could see nothing, no one.

Confused, she took a few steps toward his room. His door was shut. Now that was really weird. How had he closed it without making a single sound? Every door in the place squealed and yelped when being opened or closed. Noisy hinges seemed to be a requirement here.

Then she heard the squeak of a hinge that, in her agitated state, sounded like a bloodcurdling scream. A shaft of light suddenly spilled into the hallway. Jarred so by the unexpected sights and sounds, she nearly fell to her knees, but managed to catch herself by grabbing a piece of molding on the wall. Motionless, she watched as the light spread into a luminescent wedge on the floor just outside Nick's room. A whisper of alarm rushed through her. His door had swung open, as if in invitation.

She hesitated as her eyes busily searched the part of his room she could see, which wasn't much. There was a massive carved footboard that hid the rest of the bed from her view. The room was darker than hers; the wallpaper was dark, too, with a bold, masculine design. Though she couldn't see them from her vantage point, from the bright spill of moonlight it was obvious his room also had two French doors that overlooked the chasm.

Hearing no further sound, she inhaled a calming breath and forced herself to step into his doorway— prepared to challenge Nick in mid-prowl. Only he wasn't standing where she thought he'd be. She looked around and was startled to see him sprawled on his back in bed. She could hear him breathing evenly, sounding very much asleep.

The evening air was chilly, yet the bedclothes only came to his waist. His chest was bare, and one forearm was thrown across his eyes. His long, sturdy legs were outlined beneath the sheet, one knee thrust outward. She felt herself blush—it was brazenly obvious that he didn't have a stitch on under the covers.

Hardly conscious of what she was doing, she moved to the side of the bed. She was mystified. How had he managed to get back here without her seeing him, or hearing even the minutest squeak of bedsprings?

She gazed at him, her eyes roving over his muscular arms and broad chest, which rose and fell in slow, steady breaths. His lips were slightly parted, as though starting to form a kiss. They were firm, handsome lips, with none of the grimness she was used to seeing etched in his expression.

His hair, though dark brown in daylight, gleamed like a precious metal now. It was odd. She'd come here angry, planning to catch him in some sneaky act. But now she felt guilty for invading his privacy. Though she knew she should go, for some reason she couldn't move.

He was really asleep, she decided. She'd bet her life on it. She was positive her conviction wasn't just a defense mechanism for her unwillingness to find him deceitful. So, if she planned to stick to her opinion that he was asleep, then what—

A keening wail split the quiet, followed by a loud crash exploding near her ear. She swiveled around to discover that the door had slammed shut. A split second later, the French doors banged open, and a raw blast of wind hit her full force.

Not being a screamer by nature, she remained mute, but in her fright, she stumbled backward defensively. Before she could catch herself, she fell squarely across Nick's chest.

"What the hell?" he grumbled sleepily as he automatically reached in the direction of his bedside table.

With lightning reflexes, he grabbed her around the shoulders, but when she squealed in fright, he let her go. "Alice?" he asked in a shocked whisper.

She scrambled up, not sure what to do. At that second, Nick seemed to be the only solid, real thing in a frightening world. Her first instinct was to jump into his arms and beg him to protect her from whatever was out there, but she hesitated, trying to be brave.

"Forgive m-me, Nick," she stammered, sitting back on her heels beside him on the bed. She shivered, more from fear than the cold air whistling through the open windows. "I—I didn't mean to wake you."

He was sitting up now, looking tense and alert. "What did you mean to do?"

She decided the truth was the best. "I—I'm not sure...."

His expression went from suspicious to puzzled. "Do you sleepwalk, Alice?"

She shook her head. "No. I came in here because I thought..." Oh, it all sounded too fantastical! Especially since it was clear he'd just been wakened from a deep sleep. What was she going to say?

"While you're thinking of something, would you mind closing the windows?"

Feeling suddenly queasy, she shifted to look at the gaping French doors. "I—I'm afraid of heights," she whispered.

"If you'd prefer, I'll do it," he said from behind her. "It's just that I'm naked."

"I know." She bit her tongue, wishing that particular bit of information hadn't come tumbling out of her mouth. "I mean—I'll close them." She slid off the bed and hurried to the windows, shutting and latching them as quickly as her trembling fingers could manage.

"I'm sorry to have bothered you. I'll be going." Thoroughly humiliated, she hurried to the door. Without looking up, she turned the knob, but it didn't budge. She twisted and pulled and yanked and even offered up a whispered threat, but the door would not open.

She dropped her forehead against the cool wooden panels and sighed heavily. Nick had made no sound. Finally, reluctantly, she glanced at him. He was lounging back against the headboard, watching her. His expression was unreadable, since that part of the bed was shrouded in shadow.

She inhaled shakily. Could the truth really sound any worse than what he was probably thinking? Spinning to face him she cried, "Okay, okay. I—I came in here because— Well, I was lying in bed and heard this noise, then somebody opened my door. I thought it was you, so I decided to—to confront you and ran out into the hall. You weren't there, but then your door opened. When I looked in, you seemed to be asleep but I thought you were faking. I, uh, came over to check and—and the door slammed and the windows opened. And, well, you know the rest."

He gazed at her intently for what seemed like forever. She trembled from the cold, or fear, or—something. When she thought she would explode from holding her breath, he half grinned. "You expect me to believe that?"

Gulping in much-needed air, she dropped her gaze to the floor. "If I were you—I wouldn't," she admitted in defeat.

His low chuckle startled her and her gaze darted up to meet his. Indicating the bed with a nod, he said, "Your teeth are chattering. Get in."

She gaped at him. "*Nick!* I explained why I c-came here. I don't expect you to believe me because it's too weird, but let me be clear on one thing. I don't intend to have sex with you."

"I believe you," he said quietly. "But I also believe that door won't open until I explain something." He indicated the bed again. "You're cold. Get in the damned bed."

She was cold. All the way to her soul. At least she could agree with him on that. "I don't understand what you mean about the door," she mumbled as she walked around to the other side of the bed and slid beneath the sheet. Once she was settled, Nick pulled the spread up to cover her. He lay back down, but to her relief he kept his distance. Relaxing slightly, she leaned against the pillow and turned to face him. "What about the door?"

He didn't look at her. Placing his hands beneath his head, he stared up at a shadowy ceiling. "I told you once the place was haunted," he reminded without preamble.

She watched him, waiting for the punch line, though she wasn't in the mood for jokes. After a while it became apparent he wasn't going to say anything more. "Oh, please, not that again."

He shifted to glance at her. "Well, are you prepared to give me another reason why you came here?"

At his softly spoken accusation, she turned away and crossed her arms before her, trying to look as though his rueful smile had no effect on her. "You were going to say something about the door?"

"I was telling you the castle's haunted."

She nervously recrossed her arms. "Fine. Let's say it's haunted—for the sake of argument. If that was true, then why exactly did this ghost want me to come in here tonight?"

"Hell if I know."

She glared down at him. "You're a huge help. Aren't you *gifted* when it comes to ghosts?"

"Apparently not." He shrugged. "I'm still trying to figure out why she put my watch in your room."

"*She?*" Alice frowned. "You're trying to tell me some female ghost put your watch there?"

He nodded.

"Oh, sure." She slid to the side of the bed. "I can't say this hasn't been a ball, but story time is—"

The door creaked open, then slammed shut with explosive force, once, twice, three times.

Alice was halfway out of the bed, stunned speechless. For years and years she'd tried to force herself to forget the scuttling sounds of the creatures that had dwelled in the musty basement rooms she'd shared with her father. She shifted to look at Nick. He, too, was staring at the door.

As an adult she'd controlled her fear of the dark, never allowing it to defeat her. She was not in that merciless basement anymore. She was not alone in a malevolent darkness. Or was she? Faced with this surreal and powerful entity, she couldn't dredge up one ounce of logic to explain what had just happened.

But logic or no logic, she knew she had to keep calm. It was probably just a freaky draft. Inhaling a quivery breath, she managed, "G-good night, Nick." Quaking with fright, she squared her shoulders and started for the door. But after only one step, it swung wide again, then slammed shut. *Bang! Crash! Bang! Crash!* The noise continued until her head was filled to bursting. Who was kidding whom? No freak draft was causing this!

Fear—stark, vivid and unreasoning—engulfed her, and she lost it completely. Scrambling beneath the covers, she came up hard against Nick's chest. Without hesitating, she hugged him tightly. "Oh—my—God," she breathed unsteadily. "Oh—my—God!"

For a time, she wasn't aware of anything—her mind was too clouded by fright. But after a few minutes, she became conscious of the fact that Nick was holding her. "I'm sorry," he was saying. "But for some reason she seems to want us in bed together."

Alice lifted her face from where she'd buried it against his neck and peered into his eyes. "Who?"

"The ghost."

"That—that's crazy," she managed feebly, though she was feeling a bit better. She knew it was all because Nick was cradling her protectively against his chest, gently stroking her back.

"I didn't say it made sense."

"Why would a ghost want us to be in bed together?"

"I can only think of one reason," he murmured.

She could only think of one, too. "A ghost wants us to make love?" she questioned, her face flaming. "That's—that's unbelievable."

"Yes, it is."

When he spoke, his whisker-roughened jaw grazed her lips. It was a shock to realize how near his mouth had drifted.

"I'd be more willing to believe you rigged this room like some spook house to get women into your bed," she rebuked softly.

"It would make more sense."

His words lacked a defensive edge. He was either a world-class liar or he was telling her the truth. "You did rig it, didn't you?"

"Afraid not." His answer was resigned, making it painfully clear they were both pawns in this crazy captivity.

They lay in wordless stillness for a long time, until Alice became aware of a new tension building in Nick's body. That knowledge affected her greatly. All at once the icy needles of fear that had been coursing through her veins altered to become darts of anticipation that made her tingle with a tension of her own.

He held her close, and she felt wonderfully trapped by his strength. With a shuddering sigh, she clung to him, knowing she shouldn't, knowing that what she was doing was extremely foolish and probably dishonorable. But in her own defense, she'd been badly wounded by a man she'd thought had truly loved her.

She was angry and hurt, and she was somehow sure that Nick could ease her anger and soothe her hurt. She craved some uncritical attention and affection in her life. She sensed that he did, too—whether he realized it or not. Besides, hadn't Dean broken up with her for being unfaithful? Maybe he deserved a little disloyalty! Unable to stop herself, she asked, "Do you want to make love to me, Nick?"

"No," he groaned. "I don't."

The pressure of his erection against her thigh gave her hot, pulsating proof that his gruff denial was a lie. Ignoring both his blatant untruth and the tiny voice of reason that nagged at her brain, she put her arms around his neck and nuzzled his rough jaw. "What if I wanted you to?" His back was invitingly warm against her palms, and she could feel the way his muscles trembled in answer to her invitation.

"Don't ask me," he muttered roughly, his resistance plainly eroding. She felt a tingle of anticipation and was shocked by her own audacity. For a woman who'd never done a wild thing in her life, she was certainly making up for lost time. Her hands moved down along his washboard-taut belly, but she swiftly skimmed that tempting flesh, moving lower in search of her objective.

"Hell," he growled as she encircled him with both hands.

"No—*heaven.*"

6

THE LAST TIME NICK had cradled a woman in his arms, she'd been dying. He felt a shudder at the memory and gagged on a moan of despair.

"Nick..." Alice sighed, stroking and caressing as the sensual creature inside her began to come alive. "I need you...."

His control was crumbling. And he began to realize that denying himself for so long had been a mistake. He wasn't a man who was meant to be alone.

He'd been attracted to Alice from the beginning, and the last thing he needed was to be sharing a bed with her. The memory of their kiss had never quite left his mind, and the things she was doing with her hands were making it damned hard to refuse her. Furious about his susceptibility to her softly sexy ways, he said cruelly, "If we do this, Alice, it won't mean anything."

Her hands stopped their tantalizing exploration for a second, but then she shifted, lifting her mouth to meet his—or had he been the one to shift? "Good," she agreed, her lips brushing his in delicate invitation.

The whisper-light contact quickly became urgent and intense, full of wild beauty—like the fleeting splendor of a fiery sunset. And like a sunset, they both knew that soon, very soon, they would inevitably go their separate ways, that this was only a fleeting salve to their wounded souls—nothing more.

Her robe and gown were discarded as if by sleight of hand. She pressed against him, and he could feel her body, welcoming and impatient. He moved against her, fanning into flame his own desire. As his hands and lips touched her, a small sound of wonder came from her throat. Her responses caused a punishing sweetness in his heart that nearly drove him insane with a mixture of sadness and exhilaration. He didn't want this; yet he wanted it more than life itself.

With lingering inevitability he slowly descended her writhing body, sampling, relishing the taste of her, until at long last, he lowered his face between the apex of her thighs. Lightly kissing her, he felt her eager tremor. He was close to losing control completely now, filled with the need to savor her greedily, absolutely. With a butterfly motion of his tongue, he heightened her arousal and his reward was her gasps of pleasure. She lifted herself against him, wanting more.

Loving her hot, musky taste, he brought her to quaking release with quick, rough thrusts of his tongue. She cried out, filling the cold night air with a purely feminine sound—half exultant laughter, half moaning lament. It was beautifully tragic, he thought. Prophetically so; because the splendor they were sharing was gloriously erotic, yet pathetic in its impermanence.

She urged him upward to cover her, showering him with caressing kisses and risqué suggestions that surprised him. Yet her sexual explicitness made him smile.

She might be a sweet-faced teacher of deaf children, but naked, she was a wanton hellion, and he was far from sorry about that.

As he hovered above her, he knew he should probably be worrying about the consequences of what they were doing. But, the time for rational thinking was past. Now he could only chuckle and nip lovingly at her skin, celebrating the beauty and promise of her breasts. She trembled beneath him in her desire to please him in return. Her eyes sparkled with it even in the darkness, and he marveled at her generosity. She curled her arms about his neck and drew him down to taste his lips. Her legs were twined about him, and she pulled him firmly against her, whispering softly, "Nick, I'll die if you don't love me now."

He could feel her breasts, firm with arousal, against his chest, and felt her rapid heartbeat. She was so hot for him, her flesh fairly burned his. Suddenly he could no longer smile. He looked down into her eyes. They were filled with hunger and longing, and he knew he was seeing a reflection of his own expression there. He wanted to plunge himself deep inside her, wanted desperately to know the glory of fully possessing her, even if it was only for one brief moment.

Trying desperately to regain control of himself, he held back for both their sakes. He was torn. He didn't know if he wanted his next words to cool her desire or not. If she rejected him now, he might never recover. Yet, it might also be his emotional salvation. "Alice," he said, "I should use protection."

Her eyes widened. Then she blinked, and a semblance of reason returned to her expression. "Oh, Lord." She sighed, releasing him.

"Does that mean go ahead and put it on, or forget the whole thing?"

She closed her eyes, and he watched as she let out a long breath. He couldn't move, not until he heard her answer, because if it was, "forget the whole thing," he wanted to relish the feel of her against him for as long as he could.

She surprised him with a wavery smile. "How many women have left your bed when you asked them that question?"

He grinned, savoring the intimacy. "Thousands."

With a breathy laugh, she kissed his chin. "Well, call me a trailblazer, but I'm not going anywhere."

Reluctant to be separated from her for even a minute, he lifted himself away and turned to his bedside table. His shaving kit was in the top drawer beside his gun. He was glad she was behind him because he didn't think a discussion of why he had a gun and who he really was could be considered an aphrodisiac.

Closing the drawer, he felt a twinge of guilt and hesitated. He was a lying sack of dirt who was having sex with a woman who would happily strangle him with her bare hands if she knew who he really was.

His mental debate ended abruptly when Alice moved close behind him. He shuddered as her breasts pressed into his back. She encircled his waist with her arms, dropping lingering kisses along his nape. Lord, she was irresistible. He let out a groan of defeat even as he shifted around to draw her into his arms. He kissed her with all the desire that raged in him, all the need that clenched his gut, and lowered her onto the bed.

Alice returned his kiss with reckless abandon. She was almost insane with an aching need to feel him inside her. She wanted to laugh and cry at the same time. Her nipples tingled at his touch, but then his fingers were sliding across her belly searching out other sensitive points. She lay panting, her impatience building to soul-rending proportions, and she cried out her need for him. This time he obliged her, lowering his hard body over hers. She opened herself to him. Feeling his potent erection between her legs, she met his gaze almost shyly. "I—I'm not much of a screamer, so don't be offended," she whispered apologetically.

He grinned but said nothing.

She could feel the heat of him as he slowly began to enter her, and she opened her lips expectantly. He moved deeper and deeper, penetrating the most intimate recesses of her. A luxurious sensation of gratification thrilled through her as he staked full and delicious claim.

She gasped as lightning bolts of desire arced through her body, and she clutched at him. He withdrew only to reenter her in another exhilarating explosion of sensation. Again and again and again he thrust. There was incredible power in his surging body, and she found herself arching up to meet him, then whimpering, sighing with every delightful stab.

The cadence of their lovemaking beat in her ears and her heart, building, blossoming until she found herself wrapped in a glow of lusty ecstasy. She sobbed for release, yet prayed that this would never end. Then, at the same instant she erupted into a million fiery stars, and heard a scream, which seemed to be all that was left of the woman who had once been Alice Woods. She'd dissolved, become a twinkling part of the universe. Though she knew she was now inconsequential cosmic dust, ironically, she felt a sense of completeness.

With a groan, Nick shuddered inside her, then kissed her gently on her lips, drawing her back to earth. She was a woman again, weary and sated, but whole. With a smile, she enfolded him in her arms and kissed his passion-dampened jaw. "Nick . . ."

He lifted his head. His expression was tender, and her heart turned over in response, but she tried to squelch the tenderness she felt, for they had promised each other that this meant nothing. "You—you do too hug," she whispered insistently. "As a matter of fact, you're gifted that way."

He smiled a teasing smile. "And you do too scream." He kissed her soundly, sapping her remaining strength.

"But I'm not gifted," she finished, wondering why she suddenly felt so shy and insecure.

He chuckled, and she relished the intimate feel of it as it reverberated through her body. "For a first scream, it was damned good," he assured, dropping warm kisses along her throat.

She felt an odd flash of jealousy. "You're an expert on women screaming during sex?" Where had that remark come from? she wondered. She hadn't even been thinking such a thing. Had she?

He lifted his head to scan her face, his expression closing. "Alice," he cautioned softly. "I thought we had a deal."

She felt chastened by his reminder that the sex they were sharing didn't oblige either of them in any way. That covetous tone in her voice would have to go. She swallowed and turned away. It was okay. She didn't love this man; she hardly knew him. She liked him, yes, and owed him much. She even had to admit that she found him—what, exactly? Interesting? Intriguing? Fascinating? She didn't know. And at this moment, what did it really matter? The point was, she was not in love with Nick Street. What they'd just shared was merely an act of defiance against Dean's distrust. "I'm sorry. I—I'm new at this."

"Don't turn away," he coaxed, kissing her shoulder. "It doesn't have to end, yet."

She was glad for the darkness, for it hid the humiliation that stained her cheeks. In a split second her anxiety turned to outrage, more at herself for being stupid than for anything he'd done. "I'm afraid it does have to end. I—I'm upset at Dean and—and I think I just made a mistake. Please, get off."

"Alice," he soothed, caressing her face. "Don't be that way."

She closed her eyes and tried to ignore the glorious sensation caused by his fingers. "Get off, Nick, please," she repeated, her voice shaky.

Nothing happened for a full minute. She could feel the heavy beating of his heart against her breasts, and the seductive stroking of his fingers. But she remained stiff and unresponsive. She knew her reactions were infantile. She'd agreed to his conditions. And she knew he'd been right to make them. But at this moment, while they were still so intimately connected, it seemed absurd to think that this was only a mindless and meaningless act.

Finally he moved away, leaving her bereft. The bedsprings creaked, as if echoing her regret. Suddenly she was very, very cold. When she opened her eyes and turned to look, he was sitting on the edge of the bed, his back to her. His elbows were on his thighs, his chin on his fists. As Alice stared at him, she saw a Y-shaped shadow just below his right shoulder. A scar? She hadn't noticed it or felt it before, but, of course, she'd been terribly occupied—too occupied to notice any physical flaws on the man. But she wondered what the scar was, and if that was even what it was? She'd reached out and almost touched it before she stopped herself. It would do her no good to know more about this man than she already did. Better to make a clean break.

Withdrawing her hand, she sat up and looked around for her robe and gown. It was draped over the footboard. Scrambling to get it, she slipped it on. "If you don't mind, I'd appreciate it if you'd tell your ghost friend I'd like to leave now," she managed, surprised at how calm she sounded.

He glanced her way and gave her a grin that held bitterness not amusement. "As if she's ever done anything I say." But he looked up at the ceiling and muttered obligingly, "The lady wants to leave."

Alice peered at the door, but nothing happened. Finally, knowing Nick's eyes were on her, she slid to the edge of the bed and marched to the door. Grasping the knob in both hands, she gave it a yank, using all her strength. It flew open so easily she nearly fell.

When she'd regained her balance, she jerked around to glare at Nick. He was watching her, his expression troubled.

"Your ghost certainly has a sick sense of humor," she accused breathlessly.

He shrugged and turned away. Clearly he had no intention of arguing the point—or any other, for that matter. He was letting her go without a word or a glance.

As she fled his room, she felt a sense of loss that was so ridiculous, she refused to dwell on it for even an instant.

ALICE FELT UNEASY every time she had to trek through the castle's underground passages unearthing Herman Dimm's notebooks and papers. She headed for a new room today, deeper into the gloom than she'd gone before. Her reluctant footsteps echoed as she trudged through one of the dank tunnels, lit dimly by low-wattage wall sconces, half of which seemed useful only as the understructure for massive cobwebs.

She tried to think about anything other than the stale smell and the scuttling sounds that seemed to accompany her every step, but for some cruel reason the only thoughts she could conjure were of Nick—of how exciting he was in bed; and of his strong self-possession and well-masked fear. She had no idea what he was afraid of, what dark specter made him so detached at times, and she knew she shouldn't care—didn't *want* to care. But then she remembered that he'd cared about her. Anyway, if the truth was told, she'd been the one to seduce him last night. He'd even said he didn't want to make love to her. Oh, she'd known it had been a lie, but it had been a lie meant to protect them both.

With a sad sigh, she reached the thick, plank door she'd been looking for. Its wrought-iron hardware was rusty from disuse. She had to give the handle a hard pull to unlatch it. When the door finally opened, its hinges protested loudly. Though by now she was past wincing at such noises, she still felt a flutter of nervousness at the darkness of the room and its accompanying odor of sealed-up abandonment. Feeling along the rough stone wall for the light switch, she fought down a surge of nausea, praying that once the light was turned on, it would provide a small measure of illumination. And when it did, she wouldn't be confronted with a colony of huge, hungry rats.

She touched what felt like an electric cord fastened to the wall. Following it down, she found a switch box and flipped the lever. One dim light came on. Apparently the others were no longer functioning. Nevertheless, she breathed a sigh of relief at the absence of any vermin.

She scanned the room. It was much like the others she'd been in. There were crates, cardboard boxes, miscellaneous pieces of furniture and quaint household objects: a dressmaker's dummy, a harp with half its strings broken, a brass coatrack and a stuffed moose's head staring blankly at her from a shadowy corner. The walls were hung with everything from warped paintings to antique farm equipment.

It was chilly in the room—and clammy. Alice rubbed her arms. Though she was dressed for the job, in jeans and a turtleneck sweater, the dampness seeped through to her very bones. She wove her way through the clutter, stepping around a crate marked Woodstove to a stack of cardboard boxes. Just as she'd expected, they were labeled Herman Dimm, along with dates and scrawled notations. These were yet more documents having to do with experiments and inventions Zarta's husband had been involved in at one time or another. Luckily, he didn't seem to have had a penchant for huge boxes. None of these, though full and heavy, was so unwieldy that she couldn't carry it.

Nick had offered to help, but she'd said no—not only because she felt they shouldn't spend any more time together than necessary, but because he seemed to be one of the few people in the world who could make Zarta smile, however briefly. Maybe he was the only one. So Alice preferred that he try to cheer up the grim older woman.

She hefted the first box and flinched as her mind drifted to the uncomfortable morning she'd spent with Zarta. Nick had gone into the small village of Cliffside to pick up mail and other supplies, and in his absence Zarta had decided to reminisce about him. For over a week Zarta had refused to say anything about Nick or his past, no matter how many times Alice had asked. But today, in some sort of ironic retribution for last night's lack of control, Zarta seemed driven to force information about his childhood on Alice. She was, unfortunately, a captive audience, since she'd begun to organize items from Dimm's boxes into files.

Though she'd tried to keep her mind on her work, Zarta had continually slapped the table, demanding Alice's attention. According to Zarta's tale, he'd been a neglected deaf child. Apparently his parents had been uneducated and suspicious of doctors. They'd been ashamed of their deaf son, thinking his deafness was the devil's work, and had kept him isolated from the world on their Missouri farm, treating him like a workhorse. That knowledge brought tears to Alice's eyes, but wasn't as painful a part of the history as Zarta's next anecdote.

One day, when Nick was ten, he'd been sweeping spilled wheat from the grain bin, unaware that his seven-year-old brother had followed him. The little boy had climbed up the ladder and fallen in the bin. He was smothered, and Nick never heard his brother's cries for help.

Once the tragedy had been discovered, his distraught parents, having lost their only "whole" child, sent Nick away to a state school for the handicapped. They blamed him and never wanted to see him again.

Alice had found herself fighting tears. How Nick must have suffered.

Zarta had signed, "Though Nick was devastated and blamed himself, ultimately the desertion was a godsend. The first school he was sent to was badly run and poorly funded. He learned to sign, but got little emotional or medical help. When that school closed two years later, he was moved to Kansas City, where I worked. There he finally had a thorough hearing test. It was discovered that as an infant he'd had severe ear infections, which were never treated. Subsequent fluid buildup had left him profoundly deaf. When he was thirteen, I read an article about a new surgical procedure for people with his problem. His deafness was reversible. Through a government grant, Nick got the surgery, and his hearing was restored."

By then, Nick was fourteen, with no desire to return home. He considered Zarta his family, and she thought of him as her son. That answered a lot of questions for Alice. But not all. When she'd asked about his adult life, Zarta had refused to say anything more.

Alice felt a huge knot tighten inside her. At least now she understood why Nick seemed burdened by sadness. But was his guilt over his brother's death and the ordeal of his abandonment the whole reason? Somehow she didn't think so.

As she mulled over Zarta's revelations, she stacked three of Herman's boxes in the hallway before going back for the last one. When she picked it up and turned, she was startled to see smoke wavering before her. Smoke? No, she couldn't smell smoke. It was more like mist—a swirling shroud that occupied half the room. She was too confused and startled to move, and could only stare as it began to come together, gradually taking form and shape until it was . . .

Alice's eyes widened. Was it a woman? The face was elongated and skeletal, the eyes hollow, staring orbs. Long, wild hair billowed on some phantom breeze, and its clothing looked like tattered bedclothes that faded into nothingness at the point where its feet should have been. The mouth gaped in what seemed to be a soundless scream as the emaciated hands clawed the air. Alice couldn't tell if the movements were a threat or a gesture of pleading, but whichever it was, it was all too much to deal with down here in the dark—alone.

She dropped the box she'd been holding and ran out the door, only to tumble headfirst over the others she'd stacked there. Panicked, she started to struggle upright, but found the ghost ahead of her, blocking her exit. Gray bony hands were inches away from Alice's face, and its mouth worked in silent discourse.

Alice scrambled backward, only to be thwarted by the boxes and the wall. With no avenue of escape, she found herself screaming—her only remaining defense. Or was it merely her last, sane breath leaving her body in a terrified rush? She couldn't be sure of anything anymore. Last night she'd been terrified by the slamming door, but she hadn't been alone then, and she hadn't actually seen . . . *it*.

Nick had called it a female, but Alice had no intention of giving it that much humanity. As far as she was concerned, the entity before her was a malignant, rotting monster that couldn't possibly have any charity in its makeup.

Though there was no sound coming from its hoary, grizzled lips, they were moving. This hideous presence was threatening her—or at least threatening her mental health—and somehow she knew nothing could help her now.

Her heart was pounding deafeningly. Maybe that was why she couldn't hear the demon as it spoke to her. Maybe that—

"Alice!" Nick called from some distance away. "Are you all right?"

She didn't take her eyes from the undulating vision above her, but she realized that what she'd thought was her own heartbeat had been running footsteps. Nick was on the way. "Don't—don't come," she cried. "It'll get you, too." Too late. He'd rounded the corner about twenty feet away. "Save yourself!" she warned frantically.

The thud of his footsteps didn't halt or even diminish as she expected them to, but kept coming, louder and louder, until he was above her, pulling her into his arms. "Are you hurt?"

She struggled in his arms, not wanting to be affected by his scent or his protective caress. *"It's here!"* she cried, her throat constricted with emotion. "You came right through *it!"*

He turned, but continued to hold her trembling body against him. "I know," he said. "Alice..." He faced her, his expression solemn. "I think it's about time the two of you were introduced."

7

NICK LOOKED OVER HIS shoulder at the wavering apparition, and Alice could feel tension humming through him. She could also detect his scent—the musky scent she remembered all too well—hovering just beneath a light, spicy after-shave. She tried to draw away, hoping that memories of last night would fade if she put distance between them.

But when he didn't release her, she didn't really protest—she was still too afraid.

"Alice," he said softly, "this is Theora Percival, the castle's resident ghost."

Managing to tear her gaze from the ghost, she met his eyes as she worked to maintain her fragile control. She must have looked terrified, for his expression grew compassionate. "Do you want to hear her story?"

She couldn't reply immediately. Her brain apparently wasn't functioning properly. "Tell—tell it t-to g-go," she stuttered at last.

He smiled sympathetically. "I'm afraid she'll only go when she's ready to go."

Alice looked at the ghost, which wavered above her like a character from a black-and-white movie projected onto a screen of smoke. Intangible, unbelievable, but still threatening. She could only stare speechlessly.

"As the story goes," Nick began, "Theora was the seventeen-year-old daughter of a local shopkeeper. The castle had been newly built by Denby Percival, that gold miner I told you about. He was forty years her senior and in ill health at the time. But he became enamored of her and asked her to marry him. When she accepted, everyone was sure she was after his money. As fate would have it, she died first, after only two years of marriage." He shifted to look down at Alice. "That was one hundred and ten years ago."

"How did she die?" she asked, surprised to hear her thought spoken aloud.

"They don't know. Records say she wasted away in what doctors called 'detached melancholia.'"

"She's why Zarta can't keep assistants," Alice said with conviction.

"Yes. Fear of the voiceless demon of Percival Castle."

"Good reason," she muttered, then gave him a narrowed glance. "Why didn't you tell me about that—that thing?"

He shrugged. "I did, but you didn't believe me."

He was right about that, she realized. He'd told her just before they'd entered the castle. She supposed if he'd mentioned it back in Kansas City, she'd have thought he was nutty and wouldn't have taken the job. Not that that was a bad idea! "Well, maybe you should have tried harder."

"Maybe I should have," he admitted, and Alice sensed a note of remorse in his voice. He was looking at Theora now. Alice followed his gaze and winced as she watched the ghost's entreating gestures and the continual opening and closing of her rotting lips. "I wonder what it's saying."

"She's saying, 'Where is my sheltering tree?'" he explained. "That's what she always asks."

"How do you know?"

"I read lips." He turned to look at her. "Did I mention I was once deaf?"

She did know it, but only because Zarta had told her this morning. With a chastising glance she said, "I think you and I need to sit down and have a long talk about everything you've neglected to tell me." She eyed the ghost again. "Are you sure that's what she's saying?"

"She's been asking that same question since I first saw her."

"Where is my sheltering tree?" Alice repeated. "That makes no sense."

Nick's low chuckle seemed out of place, yet tremendously welcome in the chilly dankness of the basement. "You want sense and reason while you're staring at a ghost?"

He had a point. But in her own defense, this whole thing had a nightmarish absurdity about it. Could she really be expected to be totally clearheaded? Trying to regain some logic, some rationality, she dropped her gaze from the undulating phantom.

Taking a firm hold of her emotions, she made a quick decision and eyed the ghost. "Theora," she commanded, "I don't know where your sheltering tree is, and I want you to go away." Her voice had come out much firmer than she'd expected, which seemed to help calm her.

Theora continued to weave right and left, forward and backward, mouthing her soundless question as her gray fingers stretched and curled, reached and clawed. But suddenly, without warning, a howling wind roiled through the corridor, slamming all the doors. Alice's ears rang with the echoing noise. After a few seconds, the underground passage grew deathly quiet again.

And Theora was gone.

Nick and Alice looked around, then their glances met. She saw a flash of warmth in his eyes, but his guard came up and his gaze cooled. That slap of reality made her realize she was still in his arms, still held against his hard, tempting body. With stern resolve, she pushed against his chest in a wordless signal to be released. "I apologize for being so cowardly," she whispered, feeling oddly bashful.

He let go without protest and took a step away from her. "You should have seen me the first time I saw her," he said, his lips lifting in a doleful smile. "I ran screaming out of the castle and was five miles down the road before Herman caught up with me."

"When was that?"

"I was fifteen."

She felt a twinge of tenderness for him at the reminder of his harsh childhood and almost smiled; but she knew it was better not to dwell on such feelings. "Has that thing ever hurt anybody?"

He shoved his hands into his slacks pockets. "About ten years ago, a servant jumped out a second-floor window. Luckily the window wasn't on the cliff side, so he only broke a leg. Last year, a maid fainted and fell down a flight of stairs. Cracked three ribs. Mostly, if the servants see her, they just quit."

"Poor Zarta," Alice said, her composure gradually returning.

"Why?"

She shook her head. "I don't know. Because she's stuck out here with a ghost that keeps scaring everybody off."

Nick's brow furrowed. "I think she uses the ghost as insurance to assure a fast turnover among her employees." He ran a hand through his hair in an agitated manner as though the subject bothered him. "Zarta doesn't want relationships, anymore. Theora allows her to remain alone."

A sorrowful gloom settled over Alice. "How sad."

"She chose her life," Nick reminded somberly. "We all have to live with our wounds the best way we know how."

She recalled what Zarta had told her that morning about Nick, and her heart went out to him. "How do you cope with yours?"

He'd looked away, toward the tumbled boxes. At her question, he turned his head back to glare at her. "What did you say?"

Even though she knew his harsh tone had been meant to intimidate her into silence, she forged on. "I asked how you cope with your wounds."

His green eyes grew hard and remote before he looked back at the boxes. "Do you want those taken upstairs?"

She was shocked by his rapid and total withdrawal. "Uh, sure."

He lifted two. Alice noticed he took most of the weight on his left side and wondered why. She recalled the scar below his right shoulder blade and guessed that his arm gave him pain occasionally. Knowing it wasn't a bright thing to do, she nevertheless couldn't help but ask, "Nick, how did you get that scar on your back?"

He'd already turned to go, but at her question, he stilled. His head bowed forward, and she was sure that he was closing his eyes and taking a restorative breath. There was an air about him, as though he was fighting anger with all his strength. After a few tense seconds, he repositioned the two boxes, and then asked through clenched teeth, "Do you want these boxes in the drawing room?"

She swallowed her irritation. Clearly he was a man in emotional pain and, whether he liked it or not, she was fond of him and wanted to help. "Yes. But, Nick," she began again, "why won't you tell me—?"

"Damn it!" he interrupted as he strode away. "I cope by minding my own business. Maybe you should try it!"

ALICE WAS STARTLED awake the next morning by the sound of the door knocker. She bolted upright, glancing quickly at her bedside travel alarm. It was barely six o'clock in the morning.

Wondering who was here at such an early hour, she pulled on her robe and rushed into the hallway, planning to take a peek down the stairs. Unfortunately, her plan flew out of her brain when she saw Nick, already on his way down the stairs.

He stopped when he heard her door close, and turned back. His expression registered annoyance at seeing her in her robe—evidently it was a disturbing reminder of the last time he'd seen her dressed, or rather undressed, that way. "Good morning," he offered curtly.

She nodded, nervously tugging her lapels closer to her throat. She hadn't been alone with him since their encounter in the basement yesterday. He'd played chess in the drawing room with Zarta while she'd spent the day working on Herman's papers, which she'd moved to the library to take advantage of better light.

"Who's here so early?" she whispered, thinking of that awful Mr. Evangeline, their last surprise visitor.

"The extra help bringing the stuff for the Halloween ball."

"What Halloween ball?"

He leaned against the railing and looked down at people swarming through the door carrying sacks and boxes. "Every year Zarta gives a Halloween ball to honor Herman's memory," Nick explained grimly. "The one year he lived here before he died, he insisted on giving a huge Halloween ball. Herman was fascinated by the idea of having a resident ghost, so he decided to give the people of Cliffside, Arkansas, a big party once a year so they could have a chance to glimpse her. It was so important to him, Zarta has continued the tradition. Every year since his death the extra staff and supplies have been brought in the day before Halloween to get the castle prepared."

"So, it's tomorrow night?"

He nodded, still not smiling. "It's a costume ball."

Alice absorbed this, wondering if she was expected to be there. "Zarta won't attend," Nick said, seeming to sense her confusion. "She goes to bed early that night and lets the townsfolk dance, eat and party until midnight. I'm sure she'd want you there."

"Oh, I don't know." She hesitated. "I have plenty of work to do. And, well, I don't have a costume."

He crossed his arms over his chest, eyeing her doubtfully. "You seriously think you could get anything done with ghouls and vampires roaming the castle looking for Theora's ghost?"

She frowned, but said nothing. He was right. Unfortunately, there was still the problem of the costume.

"Do you remember the trunk that sits between the windows in my room?"

A hot flush colored her cheeks. She remembered *everything* about that room. She nodded, unable to quite meet his eyes.

"There are costumes in there. Go look through that."

She was uncomfortable about the idea of going back in there, considering what had happened the last time, but she didn't want him to see her uneasiness so she merely nodded again and lied, "Sounds like fun. Thanks."

"You're welcome." His lips twitched into a smile. It wasn't until she saw how cool his eyes remained that she realized she'd made a mistake in meeting his bothersome gaze.

"Does Theora show herself at the party?" she asked, to cover her nervousness.

"No, thank God," he said, and headed down the stairs.

Alice watched him go, admiring his masculine grace. When she realized what she was doing, she spun away, mentally chastising herself. Then she thought about his parting remark. He was right to be grateful that Theora had never revealed herself to the partygoers. If Theora appeared to a huge gathering of people and looked the way she had in the basement yesterday, it would cause a panic.

Alice shook her head and threatened aloud, "Theora, don't you dare show your skeletal face around here again—at least not for as long as I'm here." She was trying—had tried for years—not to be a sniveling coward, but she didn't know if she could be brave enough to stare at that hideous, malevolent monster again without succumbing to a heart attack.

To Alice, the ballroom looked like something straight out of ancient Egypt. The floor was white marble with golden veins running through it, as were the many columns that lined the room, each carved to resemble a hooded cobra. The columns supported a narrow walkway that formed a gallery around the perimeter of the ballroom. As far as Alice could see, there were no stairs leading to the walkway, nor was there a banister to protect anyone who got up there from falling the twenty-odd feet to the floor. However, if someone were to find a way up, they would have a spectacular view, thanks to the many tall, mullioned windows that lined the upper part of the ballroom on three sides.

She lowered her gaze. The walls were of white-and-gold marble, too, and the ceiling was domed and dingy. Scattered about the room, and looking out of place, were tall wrought-iron candelabra encrusted with yellowed beeswax drippings. Would the Halloween ball really be illuminated by nothing more than candles and starlight? Alice shivered at the idea of Nick—and Theora—and darkness. She already knew what a hazardous combination that was for her.

Right now, however, sunlight streamed in the myriad windows on the west wall. Inside the vast ballroom, the illumination revealed the dust that had been stirred by all the activity. Ironically, the little specks looked like flecks of gold floating in the air.

Though most of the house would be left cobwebbed and dusty, the ballroom would be cleaned, and according to several chatty townswomen, tables would be set up along the walls to accommodate tons of culinary delicacies. A band had been hired and would occupy the far end of the one hundred-foot-long room. Alice shook her head as she watched the mopping and scurrying. Apparently all of Cliffside was preparing the castle for Zarta's ball.

"Legend has it that old Denby played cricket here when it was rainy outside."

Alice jumped at the sound of Nick's voice and spun to find him standing behind her. She was jarred to see that he was holding a long white box with a red ribbon around it. Her question about why a gold miner would play cricket faded with her curiosity as to why Nick was carrying a box that had to hold flowers. "What's that?"

He handed it to her without smiling. "These just came for you."

She took the box, staring dumbly.

"I'd say your ex-fiancé is having second thoughts about dumping you."

Surprised, she gazed at his sober face. "Oh! I can't imagine . . ." She trailed off, tugging the ribbon loose and lifting the lid to discover a dozen long-stemmed red roses inside. A small white card lay on top bearing her name. Numbly, she opened it and read. "Love, Dean," was all it said.

"'Love, Dean,'" she murmured, as though it had to be verbalized to be understood.

"Is it a statement or an order?" Nick asked dourly.

Puzzled, she peered at him, not sure she'd heard right.

He shrugged. "Never mind. Congratulations."

She frowned at his chilly tone, then looked back at the card. Dean was referring to her with the word *love* again. That should make her happy—but it didn't. What was wrong with her? "I—I think I'll go put these in some water." She hurried away from Nick and his probing expression.

What in the world was going on? Why was Dean sending her flowers? Did he regret his hasty decision to break off the engagement? He must. What other reason could there be?

She headed toward the kitchen to get a vase, reflecting on her feelings. She lifted the box to her nose and inhaled. The roses smelled heavenly. Naturally, they would. Dean Silvanus always went first-class. He would only send the highest-quality roses. For that matter, he would only dine at the finest restaurants, buy the most superbly constructed clothes, marry the—

She stopped in the dusky hallway that led into the pantry and shuddered. Marry the—what? The best woman? And what was the best woman in Dean's estimation? A rich one? She doubted it. Dean had plenty of money. A pretty woman? More likely. He surrounded himself with beauty. Would he look for a woman who was decent and morally upright? She moaned aloud. That was painfully obvious, since he'd dropped her flat when he'd thought she was less than that.

What had happened to make him realize she wasn't the cheat he'd been told she was? The word *cheat* hit her hard, and she sagged against the wall. *After my night with Nick, I am a cheat. I've really failed your test, haven't I?* She expected to feel a terrible pang of guilt, but surprisingly she didn't. And that confused her.

Could this whole mess really be a blessing in disguise? Had she ever thought objectively about Dean Silvanus—about the sort of man he was, about his motives?

She stared down at the box of roses she cradled in her arms. Suddenly, she saw them as part of a manipulative plan. Did Dean expect her to go running back into his arms saying she forgave him for his underhanded investigation? What did he think she was—a Kewpie doll with an on/off switch?

Experiencing a surge of irritation, she pushed through the pantry door into the kitchen. As she retrieved a crystal vase from a cabinet and arranged the roses in it, she felt a strange disconnection from the act—even a growing contempt. Didn't Dean know how badly he'd hurt her? Did he really believe twelve roses would solve anything?

Suddenly, it was all too much. She grabbed up the roses and stuffed them in the trash, startling the staff into shocked silence. Noticing the sudden hush, she hastened from the kitchen, her mood a tangle of outrage and gloom.

THE CASTLE WAS FINALLY quiet. Alice yawned, but she was far from sleepy. The emotional roller coaster she'd been on since the roses came had worn her out mentally, but physically, she was a wide-awake bundle of frazzled nerves.

She'd tried to work for a while, but couldn't keep her mind on Herman's scrawled notations. She roamed the hushed corridors, but avoided the hallway near her room for fear of running into Nick on his way either to or from the bathroom. She was afraid he'd be wearing that terry robe—which revealed more than she wanted to deal with right now. She was unsettled enough. One minute she was happy because of Dean's renewed attentions and fledgling apology, the next she was boiling with resentment about the very same thing. Then, most distressing of all, she would find herself trembling at the memory of Nick's exciting lovemaking.

She just didn't know what to do. She'd fallen in love with Dean, but then he'd shown her an ugly side of his nature that she found impossible to accept. Then there was Nick, who had dropped into her life like a sad-eyed guardian angel.

He had a darkness lurking in his soul, but no evil. She sensed he was a man she could trust. And what she really wanted at that moment was to seek him out and slip into the harbor of his arms. But she wouldn't. She didn't dare.

Confused and frustrated, she moaned aloud.

"Didn't dinner agree with you?"

Alice snapped her head up to see that she'd absently wandered into the drawing room. Not far away, sitting in a big leather chair by the flickering fire, was Nick. "I've been listening to you pace for the last two hours. Do you want to talk about it?"

Even in the half-light she could see the concern on his face—concern for her—and her heart stumbled over itself. She'd had to take care of herself most of her life, and to see actual compassion, actual caring, in someone's eyes badly weakened her defenses. She had to swallow hard to stifle a sob. "I'm fine...." she managed in a whisper.

His frown deepened. Leaning forward, he rested his chin on his hands. His eyes were dark and watchful, missing nothing. "Do you need a hug?"

Her lips began to tremble and she pulled them between her teeth to hide the telltale movement. She did need a hug. What was he doing, taunting her? "But you don't give hugs, remember?"

He shrugged. "Maybe I'm having an off year." His gaze holding hers, he sat back, commanding gently, "Come over here."

At her wits' end, she found herself giving in to her need. "Oh, Nick. I'm—I'm so confused."

In the blink of an eye, she was wrapped in his arms. At his touch, the floodgates burst open and she sobbed into his sweatered chest. Not normally a "crier," she was shocked by her uncharacteristic loss of control.

After what seemed like hours, Nick shifted, and a handkerchief was pressed into her hands, which she promptly put to noisy use. It was then that she realized he was still gently holding her trembling body and his lips rested lightly against her hair.

He didn't speak to her or nuzzle her as she might have expected of most men in his position. He did nothing but hold her, allowing her to make an utter fool of herself for as long as she pleased. When she'd regained her composure somewhat, she sat up, pushing away from his chest and blinking back tears. "I—I'm sorry," she managed. "I don't know what came over me. I never do this."

"You never do which—cry or sit in a man's lap?"

Feeling awkward, she cleared her throat. How embarrassing. He'd offered a hug and she'd practically swan dived into his lap. She'd be surprised if he didn't have broken ribs. "I'm sorry. Are you okay?"

He looked startled, then shook his head at her. "Good Lord, Alice. Give yourself a break. Care about you, for a change."

She pulled farther away, hugging herself, but for some reason was unwilling to leave his lap, even though she knew she should.

He was watching her, his handsome face troubled. "So—why didn't the roses make you happy?"

She hadn't expected such directness, but she supposed he had the right to ask certain questions. After all, she'd just turned his nice wool sweater into a soggy mess.

She shook her head, swiping at her tears. "I don't know. I guess I feel like a tennis ball or something." She sniffed and put his handkerchief to her nose. "I mean—I loved him and trusted him, but he had me investigated. Then he dumped me. Now he sends me a few roses and signs them with *love!* Does he really think that's all it takes?"

Nick was so silent she glanced at him to judge his reaction. He was staring into the fire, his jaw set.

"Nick?"

He looked at her with narrowed eyes, and she grew flustered. She had no idea what she'd gotten his attention for, or what she might say now that she had it.

"I, er, really like you," she whispered. "You're a good listener and a nice person."

He snorted derisively, returning his gaze to the fire. "Right. I give nice-guy lessons to Mister Rogers."

"No, really," she insisted, touching his jaw to coax him to look at her.

When he did, his eyes were bright with both umbrage and perplexity. "What is it you want from me?"

Her fingers remained on his jaw. She just didn't want to relinquish the feel of his whisker-roughened face against her hand. "I—I don't want anything from you," she insisted in a breathy half-whisper.

He gave her a long, speculative look. That steady green gaze bore into her, and she stirred uneasily in his lap, wondering what dark thoughts were going through his mind. After a drawn-out silence, the beginnings of a wry smile tipped the corners of his mouth. "Sure, you don't," he muttered, lowering his lips to claim hers.

8

ALICE RELISHED THE FEEL of his warm, welcome lips on
her own and sank willingly into his embrace. His mouth
moved over hers in slow deliberation, nipping and
teasing as he went. His kiss was purely sexual, hot and
wanton, and she opened her lips in invitation, knowing where this was leading and refusing to allow her
conscience to intrude.

His last words had been completely true. She may
have fought it, she may have denied it, but the simple
fact was, she wanted him. Sex with Nick was wild and
exciting, yet in no way threatening—either physically
or emotionally. He was totally giving, and she knew she
was free to love him and be loved by him without fear
of messy complications. Even now, in his arms, she was
free to contemplate a reconciliation with Dean if she
decided she wanted one. Completely free.

But there was a downside to that freedom. He would
never ask for anything more—even if she wanted it.
He'd made that clear that first night in his bed.

Squeezing her eyes tight against the memory, she
took his questing tongue deep in her mouth and sa-
vored the heightened intimacy of it. No matter what
had happened before, or what might happen tomor-

row, she was glad to be here, glad to be experiencing this.

A new shiver of desire raced through her. Sliding her arms about his neck, she resolved to keep her heart firmly in check and not fall for this man. There was no future in it. Besides, there was the very real question of Dean to work out in her mind. But not now...

Nick lifted his lips from hers to leave a trail of slow, shivery kisses along her jaw. "I thought you told me once this was a mistake," he whispered.

Helpless to fathom her flip-flop reasoning, she smiled. "I thought it was." She pressed a kiss against his cheek, savoring the tickle of his whiskers. "I think we both have wounds that need healing."

He pulled slightly away and looked down at her, his expression guarded. "Wounds?" he echoed.

She nodded, nuzzling his jaw and refusing to be put off by the remoteness in his tone. "You don't have to tell me what your wounds are. Let's just agree to give each other a little tender loving care while we can...." She buried her face against his throat, tasting him, relishing his scent.

"We'll just use each other for a few more days, is that it?"

She couldn't quite sense his mood from his tone. Was he irritated, resigned or contented by the idea? "If we're up-front about it, who can we hurt?"

"You're very nineties all of a sudden."

"Maybe it's time I entered the decade." She tipped back her head so she could see his face. He was watching her closely.

"Just one more thing," he said solemnly.

She squinted at him. "Do these quizzes you give prospective bedmates ever lose you a partner?"

"Shut up." His lips curled in a skeptical half-grin. "I was just wondering if you're doing this to get back at your Mr. Roses?"

His embrace was reassuring, so she felt secure enough to show mild rebellion. "I'm not asking you what *your* reasons are," she reminded. "I'd say my reasons ought to remain my business." If she was honest, she'd have to say she didn't know why she was doing this.

"Extremely nineties of you," he murmured. "You're learning fast."

"Good." She took his face in her hands and kissed him thoroughly. "I've never made love in front of a fire before."

"Alice," he said huskily. "I didn't come down here prepared to have sex."

She had to grin in spite of her desperate, frustrating need to rip off his clothes. "That was careless of you." Settling against him, she hugged his neck. "Okay, carry me up to your room. I can forgo the fire this time."

His chuckle held mild humor. "I'll make a deal with you. You get up and I'll be right back."

She looked at him, frowning. "Me? Get up?"

He nodded, grinning down at her. "That's the way we do things in the nineties. Equal rights, you know.

You don't carry me up a flight of stairs, and I don't carry you up a flight of stairs."

She grimaced, sitting up reluctantly. "I suppose you want me to drag in more wood and get the fire blazing?"

He shifted her to one side and slid out of the chair. "Good plan," he said with a smile. "I'll be right back."

She watched him as he walked away, feeling a pleasure so intense it was almost painful. She really, really liked Nick Street. He was tender, fun and sexy, and just plain easy to be with. "You have two minutes, buster," she warned lightly. "Or I'll come up there and—"

"Use up some of that energy stoking the fire," he interrupted.

Before she could object, he disappeared out the door.

Curling up in the leather chair, she sighed aloud, engulfed in a tingly euphoria. Nick was going to make love to her again. She inhaled deeply, smelling leather, spicy after-shave and woodsmoke. Glancing down at the Oriental rug before the hearth, she found herself grinning in anticipation. All she could think about was entwined bodies, silky kisses and wild, tumultuous climaxes.

She hugged herself and closed her eyes, enjoying the fire's warmth and the heady promise the mental pictures gave. She shoved Dean and his love-hate-love attitude to a dark corner of her mind. Yes, she decided. This was right. She and Nick making love before the flickering fire. Nothing permanent, of course, but for now, it was absolutely right.

NICK WAS GLAD HE'D had a plausible excuse to leave. Besides, with his weak arm, he couldn't have carried her, and he had no intention to explain the reasons why.

In his room he removed his gun and tossed it into the drawer of his bedside table, grabbing a couple of condoms and stuffing them into his pocket.

Then he paused and cursed himself for kissing her down there. He knew damned well he shouldn't go back. He ought to take a cold shower and let her feel abandoned, rejected. For her sake, he should allow her frustration to turn into an anger so healthy that she would never want to climb into his lap again, never want to kiss him or even look in his direction.

But apparently he was more of a selfish bastard than he'd ever thought—because he was already out of his room and heading toward the stairs.

He instinctively knew she was doing this to get back at Silvanus, whether she admitted it or not. Her ex-fiancé's flimsy attempt to win back her good graces had really set her off. Silvanus might be rich and powerful, but where Alice was concerned, he was simply an idiot. She deserved an abject, groveling apology at the very least. Actually, it looked as though she was planning to hold out for just that.

She might not intend that Silvanus should ever find out that she and Nick were briefly lovers; but then again, she just might. She could unconsciously mean to turn their sexual relationship into a little revenge test for Silvanus. Something like, "I've screwed around, dear. Either accept me as I am or go to hell!"

Nick couldn't blame her for being human, but he knew he was being a perfect fool to go along with it. Silvanus's injured pride might dictate that he send his thugs to find Nick one dark night and turn his face into hamburger.

Even as his mind churned with brooding doubts, he headed down the stairs two at a time, his mood suddenly as buoyant as his step, the shadows less oppressive around his heart.

ALICE WAS TENDING the fire when she heard Nick's returning footsteps. Her heart lurched, but she didn't turn. She continued to kneel on the carpet, nudging two new logs into place with a poker. For some reason she couldn't face him. Enough time had passed since he'd left to make her feel stupid about the childish way she'd acted.

"Hi," he said, joining her on the rug. "Where'd you get the wood?"

"Chopped down a tree," she quipped self-consciously, wondering if the heat on her face was from the fire or her own humiliation.

"I like that in a woman."

"What?" She'd lost track of the conversation and couldn't help but give him a curious glance.

He was smiling at her in that softly sexy way he had, and she had a crazy urge to leap into his arms, but fought it.

"That winsome lumberjack quality," he explained. "I like that in a woman."

Sympathy seemed to twinkle in his eyes. Evidently he could see that she was uncomfortable, and he was trying to put her at ease. And it was working, because she managed to smile. "I can lift cars, too," she said, joking shyly, "if you ever find yourself without a car jack."

He laughed as though genuinely amused. The warmth of the sound burned away her self-consciousness, and instantly her heart began to hammer.

The change was so unexpected, so intense, she shot a shocked glance his way. That glimpse of his strong, fire-lit body was very effective, making her pulse throb faster. Not knowing what to do, she shifted nervously away to stoke the already blazing fire.

A large hand came down to cover hers, removing the poker and laying it aside. Her fingers seemed to sizzle with the lingering delight of flesh-to-flesh contact. When their eyes met again, the message in his was starkly sexual. With a giddy sigh she couldn't smother, she moved into his embrace, aware of a feeling of homecoming as he lowered her to the rug.

She felt a thrilling jolt as his erection pressed against her. He was letting her know quite vividly how ready he was to gratify her, and she groaned with pleasure. Aching for him, she arched up, rubbing her hips wantonly against his.

His wicked tongue traced the supple fullness of her lips. "I love your mouth," he whispered.

She smiled, holding him so tightly she trembled. "Undress me, Nick. Undress me, slowly. . . ."

ALICE STOOD NAKED beside her bed. Just stood there, rubbing her arms, her thoughts muddled, undefined, like debris from some wild storm being blown about. She caught her reflection in the mirror that hung over the writing desk and stared at her body as though she'd never seen herself before. She hadn't thought much about her body before now. But today, she stared and frowned, bewildered.

Was this cool, pale flesh really capable of the scandalous acts she'd experienced with Nick last night? She watched herself, unblinking, unsmiling, almost fearing the woman she saw in that dim old mirror. *You're depraved, Alice Woods,* she silently scolded, her cheeks growing hot with recollection. *Nobody taught you what you did last night.* Her expression was condemning, yet her body quivered with delight at the memories.

Then she smiled. "Of course, Nick should be ashamed of himself." Her gaze moved to scan her breasts. Nothing particularly interesting there, she decided, but Nick seemed to have thought differently. She turned and scanned her back, her hips, her thighs. Skinny here, far from perfect there. So why did Nick's touch, Nick's endearments, make her feel absolutely flawless, with skin of alabaster and the body of a goddess? She cringed now to notice how very imperfect she was.

Tracing her lip with a finger, she recalled how he'd said he loved her mouth. She swallowed several times, her throat strangely congested. They were just lips, after all, like millions of others. But when Nick kissed them, praised them, they seemed rare and precious and—

She flung herself away from the mirror. This thing between them was getting out of hand. She couldn't even change clothes without stopping to dream about what Nick had done to this little place, or how he'd pleasured that little place. What was wrong with her? She wanted Nick all the time. She wanted him to touch her again, here, there—oh, yes! there....

She moaned, slumping onto her bed beside her Halloween costume. She'd managed to get through the day working with Zarta on Herman's files, but as Nick had predicted, their hostess had eaten early and gone off to bed, her last, brusque sign a bitter curse for the world at large and for her and Nick in particular. That had been just after she'd instructed Alice to make sure the partygoers were promptly ejected at midnight.

Alice was not only expected to attend the Halloween ball, but was officially in charge. Thirty minutes ago, when she'd come up to her room to change, the staff had been scurrying around getting the delicious-smelling food laid out on the long tables in the ballroom. A band, dressed like rotting corpses, was setting up, and within minutes, nearly the entire adult population of Cliffside, Arkansas, would be arriving.

Within minutes, Alice reminded herself, she would also be seeing Nick again. She toyed with her lip, discovering her breathing was getting harder at the very thought. *Alice, it was just sex. Get over it!* she rebuked herself angrily. *A modern nineties woman knows the difference between sex and love and can handle it. You and Nick made a deal, remember?*

She inhaled deeply. Why wasn't this working the way it was supposed to? Why hadn't she been able to put Nick from her mind? Sometimes she thought she would never quite put from her memory what they'd shared so intimately.

She groaned aloud, knowing she couldn't go on like this. Not with heart palpitations, shortness of breath and a weakness in her legs every time he glanced her way. She hadn't even been able to eat today.

Nick had noticed her discomfort. He seemed to notice everything, darn him. He'd also noticed how she backed off every time he came close, and she could tell by his speculative expression that he'd guessed why. She simply wasn't cut out to be free and easy with sex—nineties or no nineties.

He hadn't said anything, certainly hadn't objected to her sudden standoffish behavior. Considering his tendency to remain distant much of the time, she supposed he was in accord with her decision and probably felt the same way.

Last night in his arms had been good—no, perfect. Quite possibly he was as frightened as she. Something like that could become a habit, and that particular habit was something neither of them was prepared for. She knew Nick's plans didn't include commitment, and to be honest, she had no idea what her plans were.

She was sure Nick thought she was using him, and she supposed she was, to a degree. But not for revenge. In fact, Dean no longer seemed to matter to her. She almost didn't care if he sought her forgiveness.

Utterly confused by her thoughts, she picked up a pair of tights and began to slip them on. It was time she got dressed for the costume ball. She'd found her costume among several others in the trunk in Nick's room. Those she'd decided against were a skimpy black-cat outfit, a rock-monster costume obviously made for a person well over six feet tall and the back half of a cow. The one she'd chosen, a George Washington outfit, had been the most acceptable of the lot, though admittedly a little large for her.

The mask was one of those cardboard things with eye cutouts that fastened with a rubber band. She didn't really need to wear the mask, because no one from Cliffside would recognize her. But since the costume, wig and mask covered every inch of her but her lips, she thought she could avoid Nick—even though he was thoroughly acquainted with every curve and hollow of her body.

Then the words he'd spoken came back to her. "I love your mouth." She blushed as she slipped on her bra, flushing all the way to the tips of her breasts. He would recognize her—with or without a mask.

Enough! she warned herself. *No more dwelling on something that's over.* Grabbing up her breeches, she stepped into them, hoping Nick would decide not to come to the ball.

Sure, her mind sneered. *And maybe the partygoers will boogie down to Theora's version of "Monster Mash."*

THE BAND WAS PLAYING the love theme from *The Night Of The Living Dead*—or at least that's what they'd laughingly announced. Alice was too busy to worry about what the music was. She was dancing—out of charity—with Swamp Thing, who only seemed able to do the Pony—no matter what the beat was. As the discordant melody shambled along at a somber, graveyard pace, most of the other monsters and ghouls were locked together in a death waltz. But Swamp Thing continued to hop from one leg to the other in a step-touch-step—more like stomp-thud-stomp—his slime-green arms flailing dangerously.

She didn't know how her partner kept from fainting from overexertion in his heavy monster suit. As she swayed before him, trying to stay in unison with his erratic movements, she couldn't help but wonder what had given her away as female. He hadn't spoken to her before he'd asked her to dance, so her voice hadn't given her away. Maybe at a Halloween costume ball, gender didn't matter. If one ghoul felt the urge to dance, "it" merely grabbed another—sexual orientation be damned.

As Swamp Thing continued to beat the air with his thrashing arms, Alice glanced around the darkened ballroom. Stars twinkled down from the windows high above. She noticed that clouds had started scudding by, darkening the sky. Every so often, she could see a slice of golden moon. Outside, at least, all seemed normal.

The ornate candelabra with their tall, flickering beeswax candles were the room's only source of illumination. Alice wondered how the musicians could read their music, but considering the unsettling selection of death dirges and horror-movie themes, perhaps they didn't need to be all that flawless.

The music changed, but Swamp Thing's moves did not. Alice sighed inwardly and swayed on, hoping she wouldn't be knocked across the floor by an injudicious arm flourish.

Her attention was diverted as a dragon and a gargoyle danced by. Then something utterly disgusting that had snakes for hair ambled among the dancers carrying a plate piled high with food. Alice wondered how the thing was going to eat, and why anybody would consider feeding it.

"Whew, George," came a muffled voice. Alice looked up, realizing Swamp Thing was addressing her. "I gotta—get a drink," he wheezed, as though in pain. "I'm—dripping in here. You want—something?"

She shook her head.

He nodded. "Catch ya—later. I like dancing with you. You don't try to lead."

She smiled, squelching the urge to ask who could possibly be that suicidal.

She watched the big green thing lumber away, then realized she was standing alone in the middle of a huge dance floor occupied by most of Cliffside's two hundred souls. She grinned in spite of herself. This had to be the biggest event the town celebrated all year, thanks to kind, brilliant and eccentric Herman Dimm. She was sorry she'd never known him. Zarta had lost a unique man when she'd lost Herman.

"So this is the father of our country?" came an amused voice behind her. Recognizing it as Nick's, she experienced a prickly rush of excitement. Taking a fortifying breath, she turned to face him, determined to remain his friend—and stay out of his bed.

At first sight, her eyes widened. His hawklike features were elegant and arresting, though starkly pale beneath white makeup. With his hair slicked back the way it was, she could see that he had a wickedly sexy widow's peak. Her stomach turned over with feminine admiration as her gaze swooped over his torso, shown to advantage in a black tuxedo and ruffled shirt. A floor-length black cape with red satin lining swirled about him. He was a true prince of darkness, and she shivered in response. When she looked back at his face, he grinned at her, exposing elongated fangs.

"Oh, my heavens," she whispered. She knew vampires were supposed to leave their graves to disturb the living, but did Nick have to disturb on such an unfair, erotic level? What would it be like to feel those teeth nipping softly at her throat? Delightfully sinful, no doubt. Clenching her hands into fists, she squelched the thought.

She forced an equally cordial smile to her lips, wondering if his was as strained as hers. Unfortunately she couldn't really see his eyes. The nearest candelabra was some distance away. Pulling herself together, she managed, "That's pretty scary—dressing up as an IRS auditor."

He laughed, and Alice felt the impact course through her body even though they were a couple of feet apart. He scanned her from the top of her tricornered hat to her too-big knee-high boots. "I thought you'd wear the black-cat costume. No wonder I haven't been able to find you all evening."

She shrugged. Her golden epaulets rose and fell, exaggerating the movement. "I was afraid people would shout drink orders at me all night."

He lifted an amused brow. "And you'd rather give orders than take them, Mr. President?"

She laughed, grateful that he was trying to keep the conversation light. "It was either this, the rock costume or the back half of a cow."

He seemed momentarily confused, then chuckled. "That wasn't the back half of a cow, it was a satyr costume." He paused, lost his smile and merely looked at her.

She frowned, suddenly aware of tension crackling in the air between them. Then she remembered a satyr was a mythological being that was half human, half horse.

Clearly the wearer was supposed to supply the top half—a naked torso. An unruly flush moved up her face. They both had to be thinking the same thing— what she looked like with her top half exposed.

He cleared his throat, and Alice sensed that he, too, was trying to think of a change of subject. Before either of them could speak, a pretty blonde hurried up and grabbed Nick's arm. "Okay, Count, honey," she cooed, "I'm back from the little succubus's room. Let's do it."

Nick nodded goodbye to Alice as the blonde flopped her head against his tuxedoed chest, bumping and grinding against him to the slow throb of the music. Alice stared at the woman's strange costume. It was an odd mixture of a witch's garb and a bejeweled belly dancer's outfit.

A succubus, eh? Wasn't that a mythical demon who had sex with sleeping men? The woman was sliding her arms about Nick's neck, looking up at him dreamily. Alice grimaced and turned away. Whatever the definition, it looked like the blonde had highly deviant plans for the tall, sexy "count." And Alice was sure the woman had no intention of waiting until he was asleep.

Heading off the dance floor, she experienced a hot stab of jealousy. *Don't be a fool, Alice,* she chided herself. *Nick is free to frolic with all the blond demons he wants. It's none of your business!*

She tried to put thoughts of Nick and that giggling sexpot from her mind. She couldn't stand to think of Nick with somebody else, and she didn't enjoy discovering that about herself. It was immature and illogical and—

She winced. All of a sudden her head was pounding. She assumed it was the stuffiness of the crowded room and the earsplitting noise of the band, now belting out "Thriller" at a painful decibel level.

Hurrying through the throng, she decided to escape to the kitchen for a cool glass of water. Not watching where she was going, she blundered into an orange felt pumpkin dancing with a zombie and mumbled an apology. Sliding quickly past them, she focused intently on the doorway ahead.

Just as she reached the lighted entryway, an ancient and hunched leprechaun shuffled up to block her retreat. "Miss Alice?" he said in his quiet, raspy voice.

"Yes, Jetter?" She really wanted to be alone, but the old man was so sweet and fragile she couldn't be brusque with him.

"There's somebody here to see you. I told him you were at the ball."

She felt a shiver of apprehension at the thought of Mr. Evangeline returning with more accusations or orders. "Is it the same man as before?"

Jetter shook his head. "No, ma'am. I told him what you were wearin'. He's looking for ya in the ballroom."

Curious, she turned in that direction. Beyond the double doors it was comparatively dark. But even in the gloom, she could see him, standing on the edge of the crowd. Tall, silver-haired, immaculately groomed.

"Dean . . ." she cried, her voice a low, ghostly thing issuing up from her constricted throat.

9

DEAN TURNED TOWARD Alice so suddenly, it seemed as if he'd heard her. He didn't recognize her at first, but as she stared, still too shocked to do anything, his lips lifted into a smile, and he began to walk toward her. That was fortunate since Alice didn't think her legs would move even if she had wits enough to will them to.

He was so tall and lean and flawless. His classic gray pigskin sport coat set off his silver hair. Add to that the sophisticated black trousers and hand-sewn wingtip loafers, and he was Mr. *Gentlemen's Quarterly* in the flesh.

When he reached her, he took her by the arms and his smile turned wry. "Alice, are you in there?"

She felt a surge of excitement, but it was less intense than she might have expected and was mingled with sadness—like the sudden recollection of a fragile spring rose killed by a late frost.

But what she felt most was irritation at the tinge of disdain in his tone. Dean would never be caught looking as outrageous as she did right now, and he was apparently finding it hard to believe she would allow it herself.

Removing her tricornered hat, she slipped her mask off. "It's me." Replacing the hat, she asked, "What are you doing here, Dean?"

He frowned, glanced left and right as though gauging their privacy. She looked, too. Jetter, bless his old heart, was hovering nearby, ever the gallant knight— however rusty. There were a few assorted demons, a mummy, a pirate and a rather rotund carrot chatting not far away. She felt pressure on her arms and turned back to Dean. He was no longer smiling and his ice-colored eyes were steely with determination. "Where can we can talk, sweetheart?"

The "sweetheart" bugged her. "What?" she demanded. Having regained her senses, her anger bubbled to the surface, and she pulled away from him. "What is this sweetheart business? If you'll remember, I'm not your sweetheart. You made that clear a couple of weeks ago."

He stared at her as if he saw something strange. He smiled again, but this time more warily. "Alice," he coaxed, "let's go where we can be alone." He took both her hands and when she didn't immediately pull away, his smile broadened. He exuded that same charisma she'd found so overpowering when they first met. "That's my girl. Now, where's your room?"

A powerful attraction for him fluttered in her stomach, but she refused to just roll over like a trained dog. He knew he was attractive, and he knew how to charm people. She steeled herself. "If you want to talk to me you can do it here." Though she tugged, he held her fingers fast. "What is it, Dean? Why are you here?" Was he going to beg her forgiveness? And if he did, what was she going to do?

He leaned down and kissed her lips, startling her. "Alice, I don't know why you're insisting on making this so public."

"Making what so public?" She decided not to make his apology any easier for him than he'd made their breakup for her.

He peered around again, then refocused on her. "Look, sweetheart, I want you back."

She waited.

He shook his head, appearing frustrated. "Hell, Alice, I have to have you in my life. Your past is over. We'll start fresh. I don't know why, but I've never wanted a woman the way I want you." He pulled her against him, handling her as if he owned her. "I don't care about that other guy—that Sam Bosso. I can forgive one little flaw as long as you promise never to see him again. Just say you'll come back to me."

She suddenly felt ill. Ever since she'd met Dean, she'd been in awe of him—of his power, his wealth. He was handsome, sophisticated and generous. And now he was *forgiving* her for one little flaw?

A superior attitude was the last thing she'd expected, and she was suddenly furious. "One little flaw?" she snapped. "One little *flaw!*" She pushed against his chest, and her inability to get free infuriated her further. "How dare you! Let go of me!"

When he did, she smacked his chest with both hands. "For your information, I have nothing to be forgiven for!" As soon as the words were out of her mouth, memories of her languishing in Nick's arms came rushing into her mind, and then she couldn't quite meet his eyes.

"Okay, okay, sweetheart. Whatever you say," Dean murmured placatingly. "Like I said, we'll just forget it."

"No, we won't," she countered, suddenly sickened by the sight of him. "Dean, it's awfully generous of you to offer to take me back even though I'm so flawed." Her tone was grating and sarcastic. "But I can't allow you to make such a sacrifice for me. Someday, you might regret taking on a woman with such a defective character."

He wasn't smiling anymore, and he seemed more confused than angered by her lack of malleability. His perplexity made her want to laugh out loud. As a matter of fact she heard laughter, and for a moment, she thought the sound had escaped her own throat. When Dean turned away to look elsewhere, she realized some woman was laughing nearby.

"Oh, Countie, honey," the woman cajoled through a teasing giggle, "don't be such a party pooper. Come ghost hunting with me."

Alice turned to see the succubus trying to wheedle Nick into following her to darker, lonelier areas of the castle. Even in her turbulent state of mind, Alice could tell ghost hunting was not what was on the blonde's agenda.

"What the hell," Dean growled. His suspicious tone drew Alice's gaze. "What are you doing here, Falcon?"

Alice was baffled. Dean seemed to know Nick, and for some reason he was calling him Falcon. Falcon? Where had she heard that name—

Dominic Falcon! It came to her just as Nick recognized Silvanus. He'd gone stock-still, his sexy, fanged grin fading.

Alice felt herself being shaken by the arms. "What's Falcon doing here, Alice?"

In a gut-wrenching flash, the horrible truth hit her, and she spun to confront narrowed green eyes. Was he really the detective who'd turned in that damning report on her? The report that had made Dean dump her? The report that had spoiled her reputation?

"Oh, my God," she breathed. "Nick?"

"You damned bastard!" snarled Silvanus. "Did you like what you saw and decide to keep Alice for yourself? I knew you'd disappeared, but I had no idea you were shacking up with my fiancée."

Alice felt dizzy. "Nick, no," she murmured, praying it wasn't true, praying he wasn't Dominic Falcon. Maybe he was just a lookalike, and this was a crazy fluke. "Nick, tell him he's wrong."

He met her agonized gaze, annoyance flashing in his eyes. They stared at each other for a long time, and everything inside Alice went still. Suddenly his mouth twisted unpleasantly, and he nodded. "I'm afraid he has me pegged," he admitted, his voice cold. "I lied because I liked what I saw."

"No!" she objected. She couldn't have been that wrong about him. There must be more to it than that. "Why, Nick?"

He flicked a glance at Silvanus and his eyes went hard. "Maybe I was wrong for doing what I did," he said, his voice rough. When he faced her again, his nostrils flared with anger and frustration. "But, I'm not sorry I did it." Like the sharp, hot slash of a knife, his confession ripped through her, tearing a hole in her heart. He'd wanted her, he'd lied to her and he'd used her, and now he was admitting it without a hint of apology.

Dean turned back to Alice, shaking her again. "What is it with you and these sleazy types?"

"Just a minute, Silvanus," Nick ordered, and Alice sensed his skin was flushed with rage beneath his painted-on pallor. Ignoring the blonde clinging to his arm, he stalked over to them, his satin-lined cape billowing around him. Alice swallowed hard. Hurt and angry as she was, she couldn't help but be aware of his extraordinary sexual presence. She cursed herself for her weakness and turned away.

"Wait just a damned minute," Nick repeated. "She had no idea who I was until this moment."

Silvanus flicked his angry glance from Nick to Alice and back to Nick, apparently trying to decide if he was telling the truth. "I don't know what your game is, Falcon, but I don't want Alice anywhere near you." He grabbed her wrist. "Let's get out of here."

Nick moved to block his path. "Do you want me to throw him out, Alice?"

Dean's rough grip and Nick's question brought her out of her stupor. Jerking from Dean's grip, she cried, "Yes! Throw him out!" She spun toward Nick and her tears blurred the sight of his face. "Don't slam the door on *your* way out, either!" Gulping back a sob, she demanded, "Who do you two think you are, manipulating me and ordering me around? *Both* of you can go to hell." Then, turning her wrath exclusively on Dean, she said, "As for you, I promised Zarta I'd stay until she got a replacement. I wouldn't break my promise to her even if I wanted to go with you!"

"Alice," Nick tried, "I know how angry you must be, but—"

"How could you know I'm angry?" she charged sarcastically, fighting to keep her voice from breaking. "Oh, that's right—you're *gifted* that way!" Her rage high, she reared back to slap Nick hard across the face. He didn't move, didn't defend himself, and when the blow fell, the sound echoed unnaturally in the cavernous entryway. Alice winced at the sting, but Nick didn't flinch. He only watched her with those haunted eyes.

Though the strains of "Ghostbusters" was loud, even out in the foyer, the crack of angry flesh against flesh had caused the ghouls chatting nearby to stop and stare. There were a couple of startled gasps from the assembled monsters, who were clearly not as bloodthirsty as their costumes indicated.

"Get out of my sight, Nick—or Dominic—or whoever you are!" She twisted to glare at Dean. "If we're to have a future, you'd better learn that I'm a human being with feelings and rights. I don't intend to be treated like an object—cast off or taken back at your whim." She spun away, crying. "Both of you go away and leave me alone."

"I'll leave," Dean called after her. "But don't think I won't be back."

"Alice—"

She cut off Nick's words with a sharp jerk of her arm, not daring to look back and give him a chance to see how deeply she'd been hurt by his deception. Her tears were falling too freely, her pain too evident in her trembling lips. Clutching the banister, she managed to walk steadily up the steps, refusing to give in to her desire to crumble to her knees, sobbing.

As she got halfway up the staircase, her hat blew off her head. Reflexively she grabbed for it, then turned to watch as it was carried on a sudden gust of wind that was sweeping through the foyer. A high-pitched shriek accompanied the blast that buffeted the twenty-odd guests in the entryway. Shocked, Alice watched a mummy's rags flap like a raggedy sail. The seductive succubus clutched at her flimsy costume, trying to preserve what little modesty she had left. The carrot toppled onto one of the ghouls, and the pirate cowered on his knees.

Alice didn't blame anyone for their panic. She was frightened, too. She'd never imagined Theora could stir

up so much commotion. Alice's sword and its scab-
bard bumped and twisted at her side, bruising her thigh
as the wind grew in force.

Heavy portraits on the walls flapped and banged as
the wind swooped downward, then rocketed back up.
One huge painting of a glaring, bearded man broke
loose and crashed to the marble floor, scattering frag-
ments of gilt frame everywhere. The succubus screamed
and clutched at Nick, burying her head in his chest.

Alice was surprised to see he wasn't watching the
whirlwind—his eyes were on her.

"The ghost! The ghost is gonna get us!" someone
bellowed, and more screams reached Alice. She sank
down to crouch on a step and grabbed for the banister,
forcing herself to look away from Nick. He was no
longer any concern of hers. Napkins, paper plates, hats
and wigs whirled around and around in the vortex of
the howling, malignant wind. She pushed her hair back
from her eyes, squinting, watching, waiting, hating this
craziness, but no longer terrified. "Damn you, Theora,"
she muttered. "What do you want?"

The wind stopped as quickly as it had risen, and the
flying debris fell to the floor, leaving the place in an eerie hush.

From his position sprawled on the floor, the carrot
pointed upward, his orange features distorted with
panic. "Holy crap!" he shouted. "Look at that!"

All faces jerked toward the ceiling. Floating above
them was Theora, her eye sockets black and empty, her
skeletal features gray and peeling away from even

grayer bone. She undulated, her image swelling larger and larger until she filled the entire roof area.

Alice heard cursing and scrambling from below and realized people were running in panic. The door creaked open, and the costumed creatures began to flee for their lives.

"What the hell . . . ?"

Alice's glance went to Dean. He was as white as his cleanest limo and was backing away, looking truly frightened. She was almost surprised to discover he was ordinary enough, human enough, to be that scared. Mouth open in a silent scream, he hurried out the door along with the others.

Alice looked back at Theora, who was now mouthing her plea, her rotting lips opening and closing, opening and closing.

Alice could almost read the message on Theora's lips, now that she knew what she was saying. "Where is my sheltering tree? Where is my sheltering tree? Where is my sheltering tree . . . ?" She went on and on and on as the poor, terrified guests swarmed and screamed and shoved in their panic to escape.

As unexpectedly as the hideous encounter began, it was over, and Theora was gone. But she left behind the pandemonium. A few hapless guests were still trying to flee, cursing and tearing at each other in a desperate attempt to get away from the very thing they'd come so gleefully to make fun of only a few hours ago.

Unable to help herself, Alice looked once more at Nick. He hadn't moved, but he was alone now. Apparently his little succubus had been scared out of her lustful mood and had run away, too.

A bitter smile twisted the corners of his lips, and Alice felt a twinge as she glimpsed, again, his unnamed inner sorrow. Or was there something new there this time? Swallowing several times, she commanded herself not to be swayed by those eyes anymore. She didn't dare dwell on him, or worry about his secret troubles. Hadn't he betrayed her, lied *about* her and *to* her? He didn't deserve even an ounce of her concern.

She lifted her chin, glaring to show him the strength and depth of her loathing. His only response was a vague nod of understanding. Oddly, a heaviness engulfed her. He was clearly saying goodbye.

She found it hard to breathe. With great difficulty, she managed to stand and climb the stairs. There would be no need to shoo everyone out at midnight now. Thanks to Theora.

NICK HADN'T KNOWN HE'D feel this bothered when Alice found out the truth. He hadn't wanted to feel bothered at all, but, damn it, he did.

Well, at least he had the satisfaction of knowing Alice planned to stay with Zarta for another week or two. Maybe that would be enough time for Luke to get the evidence he needed on Silvanus. Yet, he had the feeling that Alice was beginning to see the real Dean Silvanus. He hoped so. For her own sake.

He looked up from the suitcase he was packing and exhaled tiredly. It was just as well she'd found out who he really was. He'd been away from the office too long. Myra had been holding down the fort, thinking he was on an undercover job. That was all he'd told her, since he'd known Alice's P.I. would be by to harass her, and what Myra didn't know she couldn't tell.

But now that his lies had been discovered, he had no further reason to stay at Zarta's. He needed to get back to work. Besides, his first rule had always been never to get involved, and he'd just about battered that rule to dust these past few weeks. It was time he got back to work—at least until he got his butt kicked in court.

When he finished packing, he went to Zarta's room and flipped a switch on the outside wall that would flash a light in her room. If she was awake, he'd say goodbye. If she was asleep, he'd leave a note. It wasn't very polite, but he wanted to get the hell out of there tonight. He needed to get as far away from Alice Woods as he could.

There was a scuffling sound behind the door, and he wasn't surprised. He'd thought Zarta would be awake. She opened the door, spilling yellow light from her reading lamp into the dim hallway. She was clutching a novel to the breast of her voluminous black silk dressing gown, and her lips were pinched into a disgruntled line.

Smiling halfheartedly, he signed, "I'm leaving. Alice found out who I really am and if I stay any longer, I'll only hurt her more."

Zarta's brows dipped farther. Encumbered by her book, she could only sign with her right hand. "I hope she doesn't decide to leave me, too! I haven't found a replacement."

He shook his head at her and chuckled. "Thanks for the sympathy. No, she'll stay, but she might be a little upset with you."

Zarta snorted. "I don't care if she despises me, as long as she stays and does her job."

"She doesn't hate you. After all, you were only lying for me. Anyway, she said she was staying until you got a new assistant."

Zarta considered that, her frown fading, but not by much. At last she peered up at him. "And when are you going to intrude on my solitude again? In another five years?"

Nick felt a twinge of pity, reading beneath her surface bluster. "You know why it's been so long since I've visited. Brenda's death and my injury—"

Her angrily moving hand effectively cut him off. "I don't care if you live or die, you conceited fool. Never come back, for all I care!"

The glimpse of her raw unhappiness breached the walls that guarded his emotions, and he pulled her to him gently. It didn't surprise him when she clutched at him and began to sob into his suit coat. Poor, sweet Zarta. So alone, so bitter, and yet, so needy.

He'd spent so much time learning to distance himself from others that he felt as if this softening was a betrayal to himself, but he couldn't push her away. He loved the woman—the kind, smiling woman he remembered—full of hope and faith and honest courage. He ran a soothing hand along her cheek, all too aware that he loved this older woman, too; this broken, hurting woman sobbing in his arms.

They were so alike, Zarta and he, both trying desperately to live solitary, unattached lives. Humans were such poorly constructed creatures. Why couldn't they just move through life alone, doing what had to be done to survive, to live, without needing pathetic emotional attachments that could break their hearts?

Love was an insidious weed that could grow even in darkness. And it was nearly impossible to stamp out once it had taken root. He hated feeling anything for this woman, and he hated himself for feeling anything for Alice Woods.

He held his old teacher, feeling her quake with despair, trying to soothe her, but knowing that mumbled endearments couldn't reach her. So he patted her shoulder and held her against his chest as she cried out her loneliness to its inevitable end. Against his will, he pictured Alice when she'd been the one crying against his chest, and the gloom in his soul deepened.

After a time, Zarta regained herself and pushed away, slapping at his chest. "Don't paw me, you idiot!" she signed. "Now get out. Go back to your big city and your criminals."

Nick touched her chin fondly. She worried about him and loved him deeply. Bending toward her, he kissed her damp cheek. "I'll see you next Halloween, and I promise to write."

She slapped her book against his arm. "I don't care one way or the other. What are you to me? Exactly nothing!" She stepped back and slammed her door in his face.

Nick stood there for a moment. "I wish I didn't love you either, you damned, pigheaded darling," he murmured, grabbing up his bag.

When he walked outside moments later, he was battered by stinging needles of sleet. He'd been aware that a misty rain had begun to fall a half hour ago, but he had no idea the temperature had dropped. There was no way any sane person would try to maneuver treacherous, icy mountain roads at night.

With a frustrated curse, he headed to his room with no choice but to wait until the ice storm passed.

ALICE STOOD AS NEAR the French doors as she dared, watching the sleet fall. The wind had shifted about twenty minutes ago, and the drizzle had turned into ice pellets. The tat-a-tat against the glass sounded loud and desolate in the nighttime stillness. She didn't know why she'd been drawn to watch it. Maybe she was simply exhausted from pacing and from cursing a certain lying, deceiving private investigator whom she hoped never again to be forced to see or touch—

She caught her breath at that slip. Touch, indeed. She never wanted to be in the same state with the man! "Damn you, Nick—Dominic!"

She'd been teased and taunted as a child, and she'd felt shamed and humiliated. But in her whole life she'd never been so intentionally degraded. How could Nick have done this? She wished he was there. She'd strangle him with her bare hands. More furious than she'd ever been in her life, she turned and glared at the ceiling. "Theora," she spat, "if Mr. Falcon hasn't had the good grace to leave the castle, you sic 'em!"

The French doors flew open, as though at her direct command. She spun around to look out, expecting a cold rush of sleet against her face. What happened was much more terrifying. Somehow the wind started pulling her toward the French doors, toward the balcony!

She stumbled to her knees, clutching at the bare wood floor, her nails clawing at air. Bedding slapped against her as it went sailing out into the cold, wet darkness, dropping to the gorge far below.

One of her slippers hit her temple and then was swept away. She screamed, clutching at the doorjamb as she was sucked toward the icy balcony and the emptiness beyond.

With stunning clarity, she realized that Theora was trying to kill her! Why? Why did the ghost want her to die?

She screamed until her throat was raw. She clawed at the doorjamb, but the wind was too strong, and she lost her tenuous hold. She slid out of the room onto the icy stones of the balcony, skidding toward the railing. Granules of ice scraped her thighs, but the pain was minor compared to her terror. She had no idea how strong the railing was. She'd seen several disintegrating balconies around the castle, and prayed hers wasn't on the verge of crumbling, too. Maybe, if she was lucky, she'd merely be pinned to it until Theora decided she'd been frightened enough.

When she hit the rail, she hit hard. She heard a sickening crumble, felt the pelting of bits of broken mortar and cement as the aging barrier began to give way. She raked her nails against the stone beneath her, trying vainly to save herself. Her eyes stung with tears and hail, so she could no longer see. Something smacked her on the forehead, and she cried out, going numb and dizzy. Though she was trembling, she no longer felt cold. She didn't know how close she was to the edge— she couldn't see, couldn't think straight—but she instinctively knew the railing could no longer protect her, and if Theora wanted her dead, she was lost.

There was a sudden sharp jerk on her wrist, and she heard a grunt of pain. "Hold on to my hand, Alice. That's my weak side. I can't hang on long."

Even in her dazed state, she recognized Nick's voice and immediately did as he commanded, grabbing his hand with all her strength, then throwing up her other arm and clutching his wrist for dear life. She squinted back at him. Though her eyes were watery and smarting, she could see that he was kneeling, holding the doorjamb with his left arm and her with his right.

Slowly he pulled, until he managed to drag her into the room. By then he was down on both knees, exhausted. When she crumpled against him, they both fell to the floor. She collapsed on top of him, grabbing him tightly.

After a while, Alice realized all she could hear was their mingled breathing. The wind had ceased. Dominic Falcon held her securely, protectively, and she suddenly felt sick inside. She wanted to cry, but couldn't allow herself the luxury. Though he'd just saved her life, this man was no longer her friend. Reluctantly she lifted her head from his chest to peer around the room. Half the bedding was gone. The other half was spread on the floor or draped over furniture.

"Are you okay?" Nick asked in a strained voice.

She nodded, fully registering the fact that all too recently they'd done some recklessly sexy things in this exact position. Despite her fright and her anger, she felt a hot sweetness invade her limbs at the memory. Knowing her body was weak where this man was concerned, she moved off him, all the while feeling his steady gaze on her. "I'm fine," she mumbled as she sat up and turned purposefully away. She shook her head at the devastation in the room and in a trembly voice whispered, "She tried to kill me."

There was movement nearby, and she realized Nick was sitting up, too. "Alice, I'm sorry about the lies."

She didn't turn back, didn't face him. "Yes, Dominic," she agreed, "you're the sorriest man I've ever met." He touched her arm, but she pulled away, struggling to stand and put distance between them. "Thank you for coming to my rescue, but it doesn't change anything. Please go."

"Maybe you shouldn't stay in—"

"Why is your right arm weak?" she challenged. It probably wasn't the brightest thing she'd ever done, but just once before he left, she wanted the truth from him. "What happened to you?" she demanded. "Be honest with me, for once."

A shadow of distress crossed his face but disappeared, to be replaced by resignation. "I was hurt a few years ago. It caused nerve and muscle damage to my arm. I don't have the strength in it I once had."

She stared at him, working to remain angry and remote. "How were you hurt, Dominic?"

He winced at the memory—or was it the caustic way she spoke his name? "You don't have any right to ask me that." There was a long brittle silence before he added, "No matter what you think I've done."

She gave him a hostile glare. "That's very funny, coming from a man who's been playing fast and loose with my rights." She shoved a hand through her damp hair and turned away, dismissing him. "Just get out."

She didn't hear retreating footsteps as she'd expected. She heard nothing for a long time but the sleet. "I was shot. My wife was killed," he said at last. She heard naked pain in his words. "I was a cop—on vacation—without my gun. A con I'd put away came back to find me. Brenda and I were on a beach—perfect targets."

Her teeth chattered and her body trembled, but she knew it had nothing to do with her damp robe and hair. Her throat grew dry and she realized her mouth was open in shock, and she closed it. Needing to act, to do something, she moved to close the gaping French doors. Turning back, she leaned weakly against one. Unable to help herself, she looked at him. His shadowy eyes glittered with unshed tears. He was no longer staring at her; he was looking inward, back to that day on the beach.

So Dominic Falcon had not only lost his little brother—he'd lost his wife, too. And from the way he'd said it, she sensed that he blamed himself for her death. How horrible for him to carry around such guilt. She ached to hold him, to comfort him, for she could see the horror he was reliving, though he was struggling to keep the emotions at bay.

She was about to express her sympathy, but didn't have a chance because he said, "I think you should know that the phones are dead."

She was startled by his change of subject. Clearly, he was a man of great emotional control, because suddenly he was all business. "The phones are out because of the storm?"

"I hope so."

"What do you mean?"

He turned his back on her and headed for the door. Alice was shocked to see a gun stuck in his belt. Apparently he didn't ever plan to be without one again. Could she blame him?

"I don't think Theora wants me to leave quite yet," he said.

"That's crazy."

When he reached her door, he looked at her, his expression dark. "To test my theory, I started the car—rather, I tried to start it. No good. Jetter's didn't start, either."

She was speechless.

"I don't think she was trying to kill you, Alice," he said. "I think she was just trying to get your undivided attention. Mine, too, I guess."

Alice shook her head woodenly, not understanding.

"I think she wants us to find her sheltering tree."

"You mean she's trapping us here until we do what she wants?" she cried.

Nick nodded grimly, then disappeared through the door.

10

MUCH TO ALICE'S REGRET, Nick's theory proved to be correct. The phones and the vehicles were as dead as Theora. Three days had passed since Alice's close call on the balcony; three days of icy weather and an equally icy atmosphere inside the castle between Nick and Alice. She would have nothing to do with him.

Her headache, caused by being hit by the broken railing, was finally gone. The lump it made above her left eyebrow had mellowed into a yellowish-blue bruise. But the ache in her heart caused by Nick's lies was still there—a raw, primitive misery that wouldn't heal for a very long time.

Her work finished for the day, Alice walked absently to the window of the study. The sun was at last showing itself, and the ice was melting. That knowledge didn't particularly brighten her spirits. After all, it wasn't ice that was keeping her imprisoned here with the man she most despised in the world. No, it was an angry ghost.

She shook her head at the insanity of her situation and turned away from the window. She might as well start trying to solve Theora's problem. It was either brave the dark and moldy recesses of the castle in search of heaven knew what to help find Theora's sheltering tree, or be trapped here with Dominic Falcon for evermore.

She swung open the door, then abruptly halted. Nick was standing before her, his expression brooding, his fist raised as though he was about to knock. Each was surprised to see the other.

"Hi," he finally offered, with a wan grin. "I thought you might want some help digging around in the basement, considering how you feel about dark places."

She bristled. "I don't want anything from you, Dominic."

A look of resignation crossed his face. "You can call me Nick. A lot of my friends do."

"That's very interesting. Now, if you'll excuse me..." She brushed past him and hurried away.

FIVE HOURS LATER, Alice was deep inside the musty bowels of the old castle, grimy, hungry and on the verge of frustrated tears. She'd rummaged through seven mildewed boxes marked either Percival or merely Save and had found nothing to do with Theora. Unless five pairs of men's boots, seven pipes, a few pouches of moldy tobacco, one bent and tarnished silver fork, rotting dress suits and some pieces of English bone china were the key to the mystery.

She wiped her face with the back of her hand and slumped against a pile of unchecked boxes. This would take forever. She rubbed her temples, wincing at the gritty feel of her hands against her head. Nick's face came to her mind, and she stilled, tears welling in her eyes. He'd been trying to make amends when he'd mentioned her fear of dark places. But the reminder that he knew so much about her had made her boiling mad, and she'd refused.

At least she hoped that was why she'd refused so angrily. But a suspicion nagged. Could it be that she was upset because he also knew her lusty, erotic side? Was that what really hurt? He'd betrayed her in so many ways, it was hard to choose which she resented most. He'd lied to her from the moment they met, allowing her to care about him, worry about him. Then, he'd ruthlessly used that fondness to his own lecherous advantage.

But even as badly as he'd used her, she had to face the fact that she needed his help if she was ever going to solve this mystery. After all, he was a P.I. and an ex-cop. He should know how to conduct an investigation. "If nothing else," she mused, "he'd be another set of hands." She shook her head, moaning, "Darn you, Theora. Can't you give me any hints at all? Does he *have* to be involved?"

She waited, not daring to breathe, her heart thudding with hope. But nothing out of the ordinary happened. There wasn't even the familiar sound of scuttling critters.

A new sense of dejection overwhelmed her. She supposed that if Theora knew how to find her "sheltering tree," she'd have done it by now. Resigned, Alice accepted the truth. No matter how distasteful the prospect might be, she had to ask Nick for help.

NICK STOOD ON THE PATIO watching the sunset. The temperature was dropping with the sun, but he hardly registered the biting chill. Clutching the banister, his thoughts jumped from dark self-disgust to curiosity as to what Theora's sheltering tree was. For some reason, he didn't think it was a real tree. After all these years, it must be dead by now. So, where else would he look? Alice didn't want his help, but that didn't mean she wasn't going to get it.

He caught movement out of the corner of his eye. He stiffened but didn't turn. Years of experience told him that whoever it was, was up to no good. Someone was skulking in the shadow of the gazebo. He felt cold now. Not the cold the dusk was bringing on, but an inner frigidity, a paralyzing fear, dredged up from long-suppressed memories and a thousand damning night-mares.

He'd been a sitting duck once before—the day he'd been wounded and Brenda had died. He'd dived to protect her, but unarmed, he'd been unable to do any-thing except take a bullet for her. But it hadn't been enough. He'd cradled her with his one undamaged arm, cursing himself and angrily demanding that she not leave him. But she hadn't been able to hold on to life, and he'd helplessly watched her die. That was the mo-ment when he slipped into that twilight world of the living dead—the place his soul dwelled today.

As he continued to watch, it took all his willpower not to obey instinct and drop to the relative safety of the stone floor. He was surprised he still carried around that instinct.

As casually as he could, he moved toward the patio door. Once inside, he raced to the nearest window to try to see who it was, but darkness was quickly shrouding the garden. Cursing, he hurried to the front of the castle. He didn't expect to find a car parked there, and there was none. He slipped outside and, using the deepening shadows for cover, headed along the weed-choked drive into the wooded area beyond. Sitting in a copse of trees, just as he'd suspected, was Evangeline's black sedan. Noiselessly, he got into the back seat and waited.

It wasn't long before Evangeline appeared. Unsuspecting, he slid into the driver's seat, but before he could turn the key in the ignition, Nick had wrapped his arm around the thug's thick neck and jammed the muzzle of his gun in his ear. Nick winced at the sharp spasm the position caused his impaired arm. "Well, well, what's a nice guy like you doing in a fix like this?"

Evangeline made a move toward his shoulder holster, so Nick tightened his hold. Evangeline gagged and went rigid, lifting his hands up. "Falcon?" he rasped.

"Good guess. Now, why don't we go for the big-money question."

Evangeline grunted in pain. "You know—why I'm here," he said, every word an effort. "My boss sent me. Let me breathe, man."

"You're breathing just fine. What does Silvanus want?"

"He wants—to know—what she's doin'."

"She's doing her job." He had a thought and frowned, hoping he was wrong. "Start the car."

Evangeline hesitated. "What you—gonna do, man? Shoot me and shove me off a cliff?"

"Just start the damned car." He loosened his grip enough so Evangeline could reach the ignition. When he twisted the key, the engine roared to life. Nick gritted his teeth. All of a sudden there was a way out for Alice—if she knew about it.

"Now what?" gurgled Evangeline, sounding frightened.

Making a hard decision, Nick released the man, but kept the gun pressed against his ear while he relieved the thug of a 32-caliber Beretta. "Now, get the hell out of here." He eased toward his door. When he was outside the car, he kept his gun trained on Evangeline while he backed down the drive.

When Nick was sure the other man was gone, he replaced his gun in his belt, slipped the stubbier Beretta into his suitcoat pocket and headed toward the castle. A wave of guilt washed over him. *Who's the possessive bastard here, Falcon—Silvanus or you?*

ALICE WAS STARTLED by a knock at her door. She looked at her bedside clock. It was six-thirty in the morning. Luckily she was almost dressed. "Who is it?" she called as she slipped a clean sweatshirt over her head and sat down on the bed to pull on her tennis shoes.

"It's Jetter, miss."

"Come in, Jetter," she said, tying her shoe.

When he was inside, she looked up and smiled at him. "What brings you here so early?"

"That Mr. Evangeline is downstairs." He frowned in disgust. "He insists on seeing you."

Alice fumbled with her shoelace and had to start again. "Oh..." she breathed. "Did he say what he wanted?"

"No, miss."

She yanked hard on the lace, more in agitation than concern that the tie wouldn't hold. Then, deciding she could handle this, she stood. "Okay, I'll see him."

Jetter didn't look pleased by her decision, but she suspected that he would have had a hard time getting rid of Silvanus's toady. The last thing she wanted on her conscience was to cause the sweet old man any trouble.

When she arrived at the front door, where Jetter had left the unwelcome visitor, she crossed her arms, trying to give the impression of calm. "What do you want?" she asked bluntly.

He looked agitated and for some reason continuously scanned the area as though he was on guard. Maybe he'd heard about the ghost. "Is Falcon around?" he asked.

Alice flinched at the mention of Nick's name. "I suppose he's in his room. Why? I thought it was me you wanted to see."

Evangeline's glance finally came to rest on her. "I don't need that guy coming after me like Clint Eastwood, again."

"Again?" Alice was confused.

"Yeah, last night he rammed his cannon in my ear, the son of a bitch." He snorted. "Took my gun and told me to get the hell out."

She imagined her surprise registered in her face. "I, uh, I didn't know. I didn't see him last night."

The goon's eyebrows rose as if he was startled to hear that, and Alice flushed. It was obvious he thought she and Nick were having a red-hot affair behind Dean's back. She supposed the fact that they had, however briefly, was what was embarrassing her. She cleared her throat.

"I can't figure that guy's angle," he muttered.

She didn't care to dwell on his depraved angles, either, and demanded, "What do you want?"

He scratched his ear, plainly uncomfortable. "Mr. Silvanus wants you back. Told me to fetch you and take you to Kansas City."

"You came here to take me back yesterday?"

He shrugged husky shoulders. "Not exactly. I was supposed to check things out and get back to the boss, first."

She felt a rush of indignation. "You were spying on me?"

He grinned then, with no sign of repentance. Apparently Mr. Evangeline liked playing Peeping Tom for his boss. "Just checking things out. Seeing if you and

Falcon were getting it on. Would have bet a million you were, but . . ." His brows came together reflectively. "Anyway, I tried to call you from that little town last night—did you know your phones are out?"

"Of course, I know." She pulled her lower lip between her teeth, perturbed both at Dean for continuing to have her spied on and at Nick for keeping this from her—one more lie to add to a growing list. "I told Dean I had a job to do. I have no plans to leave at the moment."

He stiffened, frowning. "Mr. Silvanus wants you. And he gets what he wants. You'd better come."

Angry now, she blurted, "If you ask me, there's something perverted about the way he wants me. Why don't you go back and tell him I said so."

"He isn't going to be very happy about this."

"I'm sure he's not." She didn't try to hide her contempt.

"What are you saying?" he demanded. "You don't want to marry him?"

His hostile tone made every nerve in her body leap and shudder, but she lifted her chin, feigning coolness. "I don't intend to discuss that with you, so—" She halted, then sighed tiredly. "Just tell Dean I'll talk to him once I get back to Kansas City."

She looked at Evangeline, fighting for control, but fearing she was losing. She wanted to shout, "He's not the man I fell in love with! I'm afraid he doesn't really love me! I'm afraid he only wants to own me!" She restrained herself with difficulty. She couldn't treat anyone the inhumane way Dean had treated her. She would break off with him face-to-face.

Tears blurred her vision. She knew now she could never forgive Dean for what he'd done to her—could never marry him. She supposed she'd known it for quite some time, but something in her, some foolish childish need of her own, had prevented her from seeing the truth until this minute.

Shaking her head, she turned to Jetter, who'd been standing protectively nearby. "Jetter, please show the gentleman out." Without waiting for a reply, she escaped down the nearest hallway.

She didn't make it very far before she sagged against the wall, trying to regain her poise.

"Are you all right, miss?" Jetter asked timidly.

She nodded, and with great effort managed a fragile smile. "Is breakfast ready?" She knew that ordinary question would ease his mind, though she had no stomach for food.

"In about fifteen minutes, miss."

"Thanks." She retained her smile with difficulty. "I'll have time to wash my face."

He nodded and shuffled off toward the kitchen.

When she turned to head back to the staircase, Nick was there. Swallowing hard, she tried to hide her inner turmoil from him, but feared he already knew everything.

"Why didn't you leave with him?"

That question startled her. Then she realized he had no way of knowing she'd made her decision, that she couldn't marry Dean. Not wanting to discuss the painful subject, she shrugged and said, "I would have been deserting Zarta." More truthfully, she added, "Besides, Theora would have stalled his car, and I don't want that Neanderthal stuck here, too."

He smiled, but it was humorless. "Good point."

The sight of that grin, even as cynical and bitter as it was, made her feel restless. For some reason she suddenly couldn't talk. She badly wanted to tell him that both he and Evangeline fell into the same category of lowlifes, but she couldn't seem to get her mouth to work.

"I've gotten to know you pretty well, Alice," he said softly, "and I think Silvanus was just fulfilling some deep-seated need for you—security, maybe, and respectability. It wasn't love you felt for him. And I think you're starting to realize it. That's why you didn't go."

She didn't need this amateur psychoanalysis—no matter how on target! She glared at him. "I think somebody should tell you eavesdropping is despicable behavior—but, of course, that's the only behavior you're capable of."

His aggravation was evident in the flaring of his nostrils, but he quickly stanched it. "You deserve a husband who loves and trusts you, not a man who simply wants to own you."

She chewed the inside of her cheek. He was right, of course. But what exactly was love? She'd certainly never learned anything about that emotion from her father. If she'd been so wrong about Dean, then how would she ever be able to trust herself and her feelings?

"What are you thinking?"

She glanced at his solemn face. "You're the last person I'd confide in," she retorted, moving quickly past him.

"Silvanus is just a user. You have to see that."

She stilled at his quietly spoken words and turned on him. "You dare call someone else a user? *You!*" She opened her mouth to castigate him further, but realized there was simply nothing more to say. He knew what he'd done. Throwing up her hands in exasperation, she turned away, muttering, "I've got work to do."

Zarta wouldn't need her until ten o'clock. So that gave her a few hours to work on solving Theora's problem.

"I thought I'd look in the attic—for Theora's sheltering tree," Nick said.

Somehow she managed not to let her surprise show. She needed his help and was thankful he was getting involved without her having to ask. But she still couldn't bring herself to say anything as civil as "Thank you." Instead, she hissed, "Just stay away from me."

AT SIX O'CLOCK, ALICE changed back into her sweatshirt and jeans and headed down to the basement for another delightful evening where the walls were damp and slimy, the air rancid, the rooms gloomy, and her only companions were scurrying critters. She shivered involuntarily at the thought.

She hadn't seen Nick since their earlier confrontation, much to her relief, and she couldn't help but wonder where he was and what he was doing. Could he have really spent the entire day in the attic? "Who cares," she muttered, opening the door that led to the cellar. A wall of thick fog met her head-on, and she stumbled to a stop, gaping at the gray-white haze that filled the passageway. It gave off such a sulfurous stench that Alice had to swallow spasmodically to keep from retching. Slamming the door and leaning heavily against it, she cried, "Oh, Theora, what is it this time? I'm doing everything I can for you." She rested a hand on her churning stomach. "What do you want from me?"

It took a few minutes for the queasiness to subside, and by that time, she was suspicious. "Please," she pleaded to the empty hallway before her. "Don't tell me you want me to go to the attic. I won't do it—not with him up there."

She rubbed her arms nervously, waiting for some dire response—like the roof caving in. Nothing happened. Relief flooded through her, but it was short-lived, because a few seconds later, she smelled sulfur again. She looked down and saw it was seeping beneath the door. "Oh, God . . ." Theora planned to fill the whole place with the nasty stuff. She turned away, doubling over and covering her mouth and nose with her hands, as the putrid smell grew stronger.

Her eyes began to water, and she choked and coughed. Stumbling, she lurched forward to get away. "Okay. Okay... I'm going." Huffing and puffing, she managed to outrun the odorous mist and headed up one flight of stairs after another. When she got to the third floor, she went down a long, dark hall. Here the air only smelled musty, and she breathed deeply. It seemed as fragrant as a rose garden by comparison. Reaching the door that led to the attic rooms above, she hesitated for only an instant, resigned to the fact that Theora was going to get her way.

Like someone condemned to the gallows, she climbed the wooden steps to the attic. She hoped fervently that Nick was downstairs playing checkers with Zarta, but had a feeling that wasn't the case. Theora wanted her to see Nick. The question was why? "Theora, if you're bored, and you think getting us together will make things a little more titillating for you, you've gone to a lot of trouble for nothing."

"If you're talking to me, you'll have to speak up."

Alice spun around and saw that one of the doors was open. She peered inside to see Nick standing over an open trunk. He wasn't smiling. "Anything wrong?" he questioned.

She stepped inside the room. There were a couple of gun-slit windows along the rounded tower walls, allowing in thin strips of waning daylight. "How can you see in here?" she asked.

He indicated the wall. "You're probably right. It's getting dark. There's a switch by your left shoulder."

Watching her curiously, he repeated, "Something wrong?"

She flipped on the light, and one low-wattage bulb, hanging from a cord, flickered on. "Nothing a good Ghostbuster couldn't cure."

He frowned in confusion.

She shrugged. "Theora wanted me up here for some reason."

He half grinned, and she noticed a rather charming streak of dust across his chin. "I'll have to thank her. I could use some company."

Suddenly she found it hard to breathe. Trying to remain unaffected by Nick's seductive presence, she said, "Theora didn't insist I help you, just that I come up here. I think I'll check out some of the other rooms."

"I see," he murmured, bending over the trunk again.

Just like that, she'd been dismissed. Well, what did she want him to do, beg her to stay? Not for a minute. Turning to go, she found the door closed. That was curious. She didn't recall shutting it.

A creeping sensation of betrayal crept up her spine, and she tried the knob. It didn't budge. "Oh, Theora..." she whimpered under her breath.

"Is there a problem?"

She spun on him. "Why is she doing this to me?"

He shrugged. "I wouldn't know. I'm having a ball, myself."

She recognized the heavy sarcasm in his words, but it didn't ease her nervous irritation. "I wish you were a real locksmith. Then maybe you could be of some help."

He lowered the lid of the trunk and sat down on it. Leaning forward, he rested his hands on his thighs. "Why don't I just shoot the doorknob to kingdom come?" He sounded weary.

Unfortunately, even as tired as he was, his chiseled features were still strikingly handsome and his somber eyes were as mesmerizing as ever. She made herself focus on their current predicament, coming to grips with what he was telling her. If Theora wanted them in this room, nothing would get them out. Disheartened, she looked around and spied a sturdy box. She went over and sat down, feeling helpless. She, too, rested her hands on her thighs, staring back at him. "What do you propose we do now?"

He sat back and rubbed his bad shoulder. "We can work or we can wait."

"Work," she decided, fearing that sitting there staring at Nick would do her mental state more harm than good. She needed to keep her mind occupied with other things.

"Right." He started to rise, but stopped halfway. Then he slowly lowered himself to the trunk.

Alice didn't have to ask what was wrong. She turned toward the door, and wasn't at all surprised to see Theora wavering there.

The ghost reached out and seemed to come so close that Alice shrank back to avoid contact with the rotting flesh and clawlike fingers. Theora began to move her lips as she undulated there. They opened and closed, but there was something different about her mouthings this time. "What—what's she saying?" Alice whispered feebly.

A look of disbelief darkened Nick's features, and his cheek muscles stood out, indicating that he was clenching his jaw.

"Nick!" she cried, forgetting to be angry, forgetting to call him Dominic. "What is she saying?"

He glanced at her dubiously, then looked back at Theora. "No," he said.

Alice was perplexed. "No? She's saying more than no. Tell me what it is." Fear coursed through her. What if she was telling Nick she was going to kill them or something?

Now his expression was pained and tense.

Alice looked back at Theora just in time to see her disappear. That stunned her. She merely disappeared? Jumping to her feet, she rushed over to Nick and grabbed him by his shoulders. "What did she say that was so horrible you can't tell me? Is she going to keep us locked up here until we die?"

He looked awful—like someone who'd just been cursed. "You don't want to hear this, Alice."

She was terrified now, as her mind raced from one excruciating death by supernatural means to another. And that terror lent urgency to her demand, "What did she say, damn it?"

11

SHE SHOOK HIS SHOULDERS, frantically. "You have to tell me what she said, Nick. You owe me that much. If I'm going to die, I have a right to know."

"You're not going to die." Reaching up, he grasped her wrists, then brought her hands together in front of him. "Remember, you wanted to know."

She didn't try to pull away. Right now, he was the only solid reality in her world and her distrust of him was far outweighed by her fear of the unknown.

His brows knitted in a frown. "Theora said—and I quote—'Look not at this man blinded by your foolish anger. Look upon him with your heart and see his beauty.'"

Alice blinked, not sure she'd heard right.

He was silent as she absorbed what he'd told her. After a minute he asked, "Do you want me to repeat it?"

She peered at him closely, the words echoing in her mind. *Look upon him with your heart and see his beauty.* As she watched him, she shivered, overwhelmingly aware of the touch of his fingers on hers. *No!* she cried inwardly. How could she be so weak and stupid? She knew everything there was to know about this man and his motives, and they were far from beautiful. Just thinking about it hurt. She shoved away his hands, hating the fact that she'd felt torn, even for an instant. "That's so low," she hissed, "pretending a ghost is pleading your case!"

She ran across the room, but once again found her escape thwarted by a door that wouldn't open. Frustrated and emotionally exhausted, she leaned against it, resting her forehead on the aging planks. She wanted to cry, but bit her lip to stop herself.

Why had Theora brought her up here? Why was the ghost torturing her this way? Why was her life such a mess?

"Alice—"

"Shut up!" she sobbed. Needing to release her frustration, she pounded her fists on the door—not quickly or frantically, but deliberately, like the drumbeats of a ceremonial death march.

"Alice, please . . ."

She whirled around. "Nick, why did you lie to Dean about me? There *has* to be more than what you said!" She had no idea why she'd asked that. Maybe it was one last attempt to find a reason to forgive him. Maybe deep down she already had. She'd tried to ignore her feelings, but now that Theora had issued her strange warning, Alice couldn't deny them anymore.

She ran a trembling hand over her mouth, wanting desperately for him to give her a good reason—a forgivable reason—for all the lying. "What's really going on here?"

He was standing before the trunk, as though he'd started to approach her and then decided against it. He winced at her unexpected question, then looked away, his features grim. "Silvanus said it for me. I wanted you for myself."

She blanched. "I know what he said," she whispered, nervously wringing her hands. "But I— Somehow, I feel there's more that you're not telling me."

He peered at her, scowling. "Why the hell would you think that?"

She shook her head helplessly, unable to hold back her tears any longer. "I don't know." Her lips quivered. "Can't you tell me—anything?"

He squeezed his eyes shut, his features tight with aggravation. Shoving a hand through his hair, he turned his back, muttering something she couldn't quite make out. It sounded like, "He wasn't good enough for you."

She moved around to see his face. "You didn't—think he was good enough for me?"

He didn't deny it; he just stared at her, his features harsh.

That *was* what he'd said. The silence lengthened between them, making her more and more anxious. "So— so you decided to play God?"

He shrugged. "You could say that."

"I could also say you were meddling in something that wasn't your business!"

He didn't respond to that statement, either.

She could only stare at him, disbelieving. How could he be so blasé, so unrepentant? Damn, why had she given herself to such a man? Worse, why did she still hunger for him? Suddenly she realized her whole body was shaking. "Oh, Nick," she moaned sadly, "I could have loved you."

They both heard her confession at the same time. Alice had no idea she was going to say that. She had no idea she was even thinking it. She blinked, wide-eyed. "But I don't," she backpedaled. "I *hate* you!" She wanted to take back the words—stuff them into some black hole where all foolish statements died unstated. But that wasn't possible, and that made her go a little crazy. Love him, indeed! In a surge of self-protectiveness, she rushed forward to pummel his chest with her fists, trying to negate the damning statement with a hostile act. "You're such a liar," she sobbed, "such an immoral—"

He took her roughly by her arms and rasped, "That's right. Hate me, Alice. I don't want your love, and I don't want to love you!"

Stilled by the vehemence in his voice, she stared up into his blazing eyes. There was something hot and undeniable in their depths—but it wasn't hate. "I don't love you," she said, hoping desperately that she meant it, yet unable to stop herself from putting her arms about his neck. "I don't...."

His expression was stark with pain. He closed his eyes, swearing as he pulled her to him and lowered his lips to hers.

His kiss was rough and furious, holding her captive with its wild hunger. With punishing sweetness his tongue began a deep, aching exploration of her mouth.

There was a savageness in his ardor that took away Alice's breath, and she clung to him.

She moaned, running her hands through the thick silkiness of his hair, tasting his passion and his rage with equal delight; and wanting more—wanting the same thrilling, punishing thrusts deep inside her. Lifting her mouth from his, she begged. "Nick. Nick, please."

He gazed at her, his expression grave, his eyes glowing with desire. "What?" he demanded, his voice husky with need.

She smiled, powerless to fight her attraction for him any longer. "Oh, Lord. I'm crazy, but I want you so badly."

He didn't look any happier than she felt, but nodded in bleak understanding, sweeping her into his arms. "Damn, I know. *Damn . . .*"

He lowered her on to a pile of blankets in a far corner of the room. "I saw these here earlier," he said, "but I didn't think—"

"Let's not think," she interrupted, tugging his shirt from his belt. She knew she would regret this tomorrow, but right now, she wanted nothing more than to have Nick bring her to a glorious, screaming climax.

Their clothes were discarded like autumn leaves, quickly and quietly fluttering to the floor. And then there was nothing between them, and they were free to abandon themselves to pure, satisfying lust.

Her cries of delight mingled with his groans of pleasure, and her body throbbed with a burning sweetness. She knew that he was driving her delightfully insane and she cried out her need for him to be inside her. She reached down to caress his erection, taking him between her hands, begging, urging him to fill her.

With one more dizzying kiss, he moved to do her bidding as she continued to hold him. How precious this intimacy was between them, so wickedly sweet, so divinely indecent. She quivered there, in anticipation, her lips forming a soundless "oh" as she opened herself to him.

She looked into his eyes then. He was so handsome, his intense gaze raking her with a fierce possessiveness. Her heart leaped, and she suddenly admitted that she'd been longing to see that look for a very long time. God, did he really care for her? She felt tears of hope and joy well up, and she cried out, "Oh, Nick, please . . ."

He entered her then. Fire bolts of heightened desire raced through her, and she arched up to meet him, wrapping her legs around his taut buttocks, relishing the wondrous feeling. She instinctively began to move with him, her body convulsing with each deepening plunge.

"Nick, oh, Nick, I'm—"

"I know," he murmured, then thrust so deep, she thought she would split in two. She screamed, arching backward, quaking violently, her eyes wide, yet unseeing.

She abandoned herself to the spiraling orgasm, experiencing wave after delicious wave of release.

He quivered inside her, finding his own release. With a guttural moan, he pulled her against him and kissed her shoulder. Though spent, she lifted her arms to encircle his wide back, relishing their mutual climax.

Kissing his damp jaw she snuggled against him, content to hold him and be held by him, thinking how nice it would be to remain blanketed by his potent, gorgeous body forever. Inhaling his musky scent, she smiled tremulously, suddenly aware that a strange, wondrous sense of peace had settled over her—a kind of peace she'd never experienced before.

Nick stirred, and she nuzzled his chin. When he cursed, her eyes flew open and she stiffened with concern.

"Damn it to hell," he ground out. "I didn't wear protection."

She winced inwardly. She hadn't given it a single thought, either.

He was lifting himself away from her, and she realized with some surprise that she felt more distress over losing his closeness than the fact that he hadn't worn a condom. "Nick," she whispered, trying to soothe him. "It's okay, really. I'm not sick or anything. I just had an insurance physical—"

"It's not that. I know you're healthy. So am I." He shook his head regretfully. "Damn it. I make it a rule never to lose control, Alice, and I lost it tonight."

She touched his face fondly. "You're only human."

"Hell." He let out a bitter chuckle. "Isn't it interesting that when anybody says, 'You're only human,' it means, 'You've screwed up'?" He pursed his lips, looking irritated with himself. "Pardon the pun." Lowering his head, he kissed her briefly, as though he couldn't help himself, then sat up, running both hands roughly through his hair.

With his abrupt departure, all the pleasure that had infused her body was gone. She struggled to sit up and placed a comforting hand on his thigh. She wasn't willing to completely relinquish the intimacy they'd just shared. "People do make mistakes, Nick," she offered softly.

His expression was brooding. "Believe me, Alice, I know all about making mistakes." When he met her gaze, she saw anguish flickering there. "What if this one got you pregnant?"

She experienced a sense of loss at his angry tone. Apparently what she'd thought had been a look of possessiveness in his eyes while they were making love had been nothing of the sort. Nick had no intention of forging any long-term relationship with her. "You weren't alone in this," she said, struggling to maintain a facade of calm. "Half the responsibility is mine."

He laughed harshly. "That's my point, the other half is mine, and I'm not in the market for a relationship."

She listened with growing dismay. Suddenly, she was struck by a brutal irony. Dean hadn't wanted children, and that had been fine with her. But now that the possibility existed that she might be pregnant, she found the idea of children to be quite lovely. That was certainly ironic—considering she was supposed to despise this man. If she hadn't been so miserable, she might have laughed.

Reluctantly she removed her hand from his leg. There was no point in prolonging his agony with her unwelcome touch. "Then I guess you'll never know if I'm pregnant or not, will you?" she managed faintly.

Her body was weak from their recent and wonderful physical exertion, and she had some difficulty standing. When he reached to assist her, she avoided him. His eyes sought hers but she lowered her lashes quickly to hide any telltale hurt.

There was a dismal silence while she dressed, berating herself inwardly for her fumble-fingeredness. She didn't hear any other movement and didn't dare turn to see what he might be doing. Why punish herself with another glimpse of his potent body?

As soon as she was dressed, she moved on shaky legs to the door. It opened easily, and muttering a curse at Theora, she hurriedly left the room.

ALICE JUMPED AT THE sound of an unfamiliar jangling, dropping the paper she was filing. It only took her a second to identify it, though. The phone was ringing. She hurried over and picked it up. "Hello . . ." Her salutation faded away. *The phone worked!* She stood there gaping at the receiver. Theora had stopped interfering with the phones. Why? Before she could think about it any longer, she realized a male voice was calling loudly through the receiver, trying to get her attention.

She put the receiver to her ear. "I'm sorry to keep you waiting."

Alice could hardly keep her mind on what the caller was telling her. Apparently he was answering Zarta's advertisement for an assistant.

"Uh, er, your qualifications sound very good, Mr.—" she tried desperately to recall his name "—Thomas. I'm sure Mrs. Dimm will want to speak with you. Thursday afternoon would be fine. Once you get to Cliffside, anybody can direct you to the castle." She almost added, "And they'll also be happy to tell you about the ghost who haunts it." She hoped he didn't let little things like a murderous, voyeuristic ghost bother him.

When she hung up, she took the information to Zarta, who was characteristically negative about the news, signing brusquely, "A man! Never. I'll not have a man here!"

Alice tried to keep frustration from her expression as she explained, "He's a retired English professor with a publishing background, and a widower whose wife was deaf. So, he's an expert in signing."

Zarta scowled, her eyes little black jets of animosity.

Alice went on: "I've given him an appointment for the day after tomorrow. You many find that not many people will apply."

Zarta snorted and crossed her arms as she always did when she knew someone else was right, but adamantly refused to admit it. Nodding, Alice pivoted to go, then turned back. "Do you suppose the cars work?" she signed. "If they do, then Jetter might go into town for supplies. We're—"

Zarta slammed her hand down on the table, then signed, "The cars work, and Jetter has already gone to town."

Alice was startled. "When did everything get back to normal?"

"I don't know. Nick came in to tell me about the cars before he left this morning."

Alice watched carefully as Zarta signed, but she couldn't quite believe her eyes. "Nick's gone? Where?"

"Back to Kansas City, naturally. And, I say, good riddance!"

Nick had left? Just like that?

Without giving her employer another thought or glance, she ran from the parlor and down the hallway to the kitchen. She startled the cook and several of the servants as she rushed through the scrubbed room that smelled of pine cleaner and simmering stew. She threw open the door that led to the side parking area to see that no cars were there.

Nick was really gone.

In a daze, she stepped out onto the small stone porch and allowed the door to swing shut behind her. The sun was warm on the stones, but even so, she tugged at the lapels of her jacket, feeling a chill creep along her spine.

Down deep, she supposed she understood his hasty departure. He had seen her love for him in her eyes. That would send any man who rejected commitments and relationships running for the nearest exit. She hugged herself and sat down on the top step, wondering why Theora had let him leave when the mystery of the sheltering tree wasn't solved.

She leaned forward to rest her head in her hands. She was completely baffled as to why Theora was acting so irrationally. A wry laugh gurgled in her throat. Theora was a ghost, for heaven's sake. There was nothing *rational* about her!

What was *irrational* was falling in love with a man who'd lied about you so he could bed you.

AT THE END OF THE WEEK, Alice left Zarta in the capable hands of her new assistant, Tyler Thomas, a robust widower with an unquenchable cheerfulness. As she left the castle, Tyler was throwing open curtains and ordering maids and servants to get the place looking more like a home, not a mortuary! He was a friendly, attractive man, and Alice was glad he was the only person who'd answered the ad. Though Zarta fought his boisterous cheer at every turn, Alice had a feeling that Tyler would win in the end, and the two would form a deep friendship.

She'd earned enough working for Zarta to pay her rent through December, and had been assured by the school where she'd been employed before, that there would be a position available after the first of the year. Apparently, one of the other instructors was leaving to get married. Alice felt a little twinge at that—she'd left to get married, too.

The days crawled by. Alice kept herself busy by ti-
dying up her apartment and getting rid of anything that
reminded her of Dean Silvanus, including the painting
of Dean's hideous dog. It was easy to see how she'd
fooled herself into believing she was in love with Dean.
He'd represented everything respected and secure,
which was what she'd wanted since childhood.

She smiled sadly at the thought. Lord, how wrong
she'd been about her feelings for Dean. She'd patiently
explained that to him several times since her return, but
he still sent roses and candy. She'd run out of neigh-
bors to pass them on to, and they kept coming. Dean
could be quite charming when he tried, but his efforts
just weren't impressing her anymore.

That morning, she'd received Mort Hobart's written
report in the mail. Toying with it, she mused about
everything that had happened to her since she'd hired
him. Most important, she'd discovered what love really was—a deep caring for someone that came quietly, even stealthily, when you least expected it.

For Alice it was the great peace and wholeness that
came when Nick took her lovingly into his arms and
just let her cry. Love was quite simple, really, but not
necessarily easy. Especially when the man she loved
didn't want anything to do with love.

So, she'd also discovered that love could be painful
and lonely, too. And that led her to understand Nick's
reluctance to become involved again. To lose someone
you love was surely the greatest tragedy in life.

Sighing dejectedly, Alice absently scanned Hobart's report. His investigation exonerated her, confirming her story that she'd never heard of Sam "The Scam" Bosso. Mort reported that Scam had been shacked up with his long-time girlfriend and hiding from his bookies thirty miles from Kansas City, during Nick's entire investigation of her. Unfortunately, he couldn't explain why Nick had lied about her. And that was the one question she truly wanted an answer to.

Rising from her chair, she walked into her tiny kitchen and dropped Hobart's report into her trash can, on top of the roses Dean had sent yesterday. The report was no longer important to her. It didn't matter what Dean thought anymore, either. It only mattered that Nick had lied about her and then rejected her—and that she still cared about him.

She leaned against her tile counter, hanging her head. She could never bring herself to initiate legal proceedings against Nick. She couldn't explain why, but she simply didn't believe he was unethical or irresponsible. Even if he was a total scumbag, she no longer wanted revenge.

Maybe that was part of being in love, too. Caring too much to want to see the other person harmed, no matter what they might have done. Besides, if she sued him, she'd have to face him in court, and by then, she'd be too pregnant to hide it from him.

A new rush of nausea made her gag, and she hurried to the bathroom. No, Nick would never know that his loss of control had done what he'd most feared. She had no intention of holding a man by blackmailing him with baby booties.

12

ALICE AWOKE EARLY on the morning of November 20 with an odd feeling of foreboding. She tried to shake it off, but it clung to her like a shroud. Today was supposed to have been her wedding day.

Not wanting to dwell on that, she turned her thoughts to Theora. She'd spent almost as much time brooding about the ghost as she had about Nick. It had been eerie the way Theora had gone quiet after Nick left. It was almost as though she'd given up. For some reason, that depressed Alice, and left her feeling a curious kinship with the pitiful spirit.

After brewing some tea to help ease her queasy stomach, she went to her mailbox to pick up her morning paper and noticed a letter wedged in beside it. Sticking the newspaper under one arm, she walked back up the two flights of stairs to her apartment, slitting the letter open with a finger.

Inside the apartment again, she flicked on the TV, hoping the incessant chatter on the morning show would help distract her. Then she opened the envelope to find one folded sheet of paper. As she lifted it out, something fluttered to the floor. It was her check to Mort Hobart for his investigative services.

Wondering why her money had been returned, she read the enclosed note. "Alice," it began. "The least I could do was pay Hobart's bill. After all, I caused the trouble." It was signed, simply, "Nick Falcon." She sat down hard on the chair and let the note slip from her fingers onto the table. She swallowed hard several times, trying to keep a grip on her emotions. The note was certainly short and to the point, but what else had she expected?

She didn't know if she was grateful that he was accepting responsibility for the bill or if she was furious with him for thinking mere money would free him from any liability.

A scream of frustration welling at the back of her throat, she turned to the TV, determined to force thoughts of Nick from her mind.

What she saw and heard stopped her dead. " ... arrested moments ago. Silvanus is a prominent businessman and philanthropist. According to Detective Luke Keegan, the big break in the case occurred when..." As the helmet-haired reporter spoke, a handcuffed Dean was being led into city hall by a burly police detective. She gaped at the screen, hearing only scattered words and phrases—"underworld connections," "racketeering" and "drug charges." "Oh my God ..." she whispered, as the report ended.

She sat there for a moment, stunned to discover that beneath his charismatic facade, Dean was a crook and a thug and a drug baron. She couldn't believe it! Apparently it had come as quite a surprise to Kansas City, too, considering the attention his arrest was receiving.

She shivered, thinking what a horror her wedding day would have turned into if Nick hadn't lied—

The revelation hit her full force. Light-headed with astonishment, her gaze went to Nick's letter. Could Nick have lied to protect her? He was an ex-cop. He might have known about the investigation into Silvanus's business practices. Of course! It had to be that!

She recalled his saying, "I didn't think he was good enough for you." Now she understood what he'd meant and realized why he couldn't tell her the truth.

She ran a shaky hand through her hair. It had taken years, but she'd dragged herself up out of the humiliation and degradation of being the Dummy's Daughter. She cringed at the ugly memories and at how close she'd come to being the object of sneers and ridicule— again.

Experiencing a sudden rush of gratitude, she ran to the living room and grabbed up the telephone receiver. She had to call Nick and thank him. But as she thumbed through the directory for his office number, she stilled. Could she bear to hear his voice again? Would there be long pauses in the conversation—pauses that told her he still regretted losing control and was loathe to have anything more to do with her? Could she stand that? She recalled his eyes the last time she'd seen him, glittering with guilt and repudiation. He didn't want her thanks, didn't want to ever talk to her again. Her throat ached with defeat.

Slowly, she replaced the receiver and closed the phone book. She'd write him a nice note—short and to the point—just like his.

She bit her lip until it throbbed. Getting up, she moved without thought, knowing her love for Nick was hopeless. She had no idea how much time passed, but after a while she found herself sitting on her couch, leafing through a book. Her glance fell on a line from Harry Emerson Fosdick and she read it aloud: "'He who cannot find footing cannot go forward.'"

She slumped against the cushions and closed her eyes. Even in her desolation, she knew she was taking those first steps toward solid emotional ground—at least where Dean was concerned. With his arrest, she could at last understand why he was obsessed about having her. It was clearly a twisted attempt to redeem himself by possessing someone above reproach.

She lay there for a long time, her breathing shallow, until finally she felt sufficiently restored to lift her head. She couldn't just lie there and feel sorry for herself for the rest of her life. But she didn't know quite what to do. Her job didn't start for over a month.

She thought of Zarta. No, she had her cheery Mr. Thomas to keep her busy. Zarta didn't need—

Theora! Theora's puzzle still needed solving. The poor ghost had wanted Alice's help and she'd failed her. At least working on Theora's problem would keep her mind off Nick for a time, and if she found the answer, it would give her a feeling of accomplishment.

Her plan of action determined, she set about packing a suitcase and renting a compact car. She knew she was doing the right thing.

WHEN JETTER ANSWERED her knock, his expression was so pleased it was comical. She couldn't help but smile at him. "Hi," she said. "Where's Zarta?"

When he was able to close his mouth, he gulped a couple of times, then managed, "Why, she's out in the garden walking with Mr. Thomas, miss."

Alice was startled to hear that. "He got her to go outside?"

Jetter smiled again. "Yes, miss. I don't think she hates him as much as she pretends."

Alice nodded. "I think you're right." She set down her bag and switched to the subject that had brought her there. "Jetter, do you think Zarta would mind if I visited for a few days?"

He blinked, then grinned as wickedly as all his wrinkles would allow. "She may not admit it, but I know she would be pleased to see you."

"Thanks. I'll go get settled and see her at dinner."

"I'll tell Cook to add another plate."

Wanting to start working on Theora's riddle right away, she plucked up her suitcase. "When Zarta comes in, please tell her I'm here. I'll explain everything at dinner."

"Yes, miss."

She rushed up the stairs and bounded over the last step before she saw him. He was watching her, his green eyes guarded, every line of his body tense.

She was still ten feet away from him, but just seeing him created such an intense reaction that she stumbled to a halt. "Nick? What are you doing here?"

"I could ask you the same thing." He crossed his arms over his chest, eyeing her levelly. "Did you forget something?"

She winced at his detached tone, yet in his eyes, she could still glimpse some caring. She decided to be honest. He deserved that much, considering what he'd done for her. "I'm here to help Theora find her sheltering tree."

His expression changed from wary to skeptical. "You're getting involved with a ghost's problems?" he asked. "What in hell for?"

Disconcerted by his cynical demeanor, she blurted, "*You* should talk about getting involved!" Damn him! She missed the smiling, gentle Nick she'd grown to—

Hating the turn of her thoughts, she snatched up her bag and headed toward her room. "You're the control freak around here!" she added sarcastically.

She reached the door and flung it open before she turned on him, deciding it was time he faced a few facts. "Nick, you can't control everything in life. You'll kill yourself trying." She inhaled deeply in an effort to still the tremor in her voice. "What happened to your brother and your wife wasn't your fault."

For an instant he looked stricken, then a bitter smile tugged at the corners of his mouth. "I feel much better now. Thanks."

"Okay. *Don't* listen to me. It's your life," she snapped, forcing herself to look away from the lingering pain in his eyes. "Wallow in guilt, if it pleases you. I have work to do."

She marched into her room, slamming the door. Full of frustration, rage and hopelessness, she flung her bag on the bed. It bounced, then hit the wall before it crashed to the floor. "Why did you have to be here?" she moaned. She felt a surge of nausea, but took several deep breaths and fought it down. The last thing she needed was to have to dash for the bathroom in front of him.

Maybe it would help to lie down for a few minutes. Light-headed, she sank down onto the damask bedspread. Just before she closed her eyes, she noticed that a piece of wallpaper had curled away from the wall next to the headboard. It must have been knocked loose by her suitcase. She felt a twinge of guilt for having damaged something that didn't belong to her. Sliding over, she took hold of the loose corner of wallpaper, wondering how she could reattach it.

She cocked her head to get a better view. Where the wallpaper had come loose she could see that there was a crack in the old, gray plaster. She touched it apprehensively, hoping she hadn't ruined that, too.

She tugged on the antique wallpaper, revealing more plaster. Soon she could see a network of larger cracks and then a space about two inches deep and seven inches square was exposed.

Alice gasped. A leather-bound book was wedged into the opening. Her heart went to her throat as she lifted it out and read the words embossed in golden script on the cover: "Diary of Theora Percival."

Evidently, Theora had chiseled out a cavity large enough to hide her journal. Alice examined the edge of the wallpaper and noticed that it was discolored and sticky in places. Fearing that the diary would be discovered, Theora must have used some kind of glue to seal it behind the wallpaper.

Hardly daring to believe her luck, she opened the journal and read the first page. The writing was uneven, and the ink was faded, but it was clear enough. Could Theora's diary tell her what the sheltering tree might be?

With shaking fingers, she touched the fragile pages and traced the leather binder. "Is this where the answer lies, Theora?" she whispered. She looked up, casting her gaze about the room, but all remained quiet. With a resigned sigh, she wriggled back to sit against the headboard, and began to read.

There was a tap at her door. Her head came up and her heart began to race. It had only been a few minutes since she'd slammed her door in a huff. It couldn't be anyone else but Nick. Hoping she was wrong, she called, "Who's there?" The words wavered, and she sucked in a breath, trying to calm herself.

"Alice, you don't sound well. Did you fall?"

He must have heard her suitcase crash to the floor. When he hadn't heard anything more, he'd decided to check on her. How neighborly of him! "I wouldn't get involved, if I were you," she croaked, wincing at the strangled sound of her voice.

The door opened. After one look at her, his apprehensive expression dissolved into one of relief. "I thought you'd broken your neck."

She didn't respond, fearful her voice might fail her completely. In self-defense, she returned her gaze to the diary, wondering why Mr. Noninvolvement was lingering.

"What happened to the wall?"

She could hear his approach and felt a tingle of anxiety rush along her spine. "Go away," she managed.

He examined the wallpaper and then the hole in the plaster. Since he was a dangerously bright man, Alice wasn't surprised when he said, "You found Theora's diary?"

She swallowed and turned a page.

The bed moved and the springs squeaked, making it alarmingly clear that he'd joined her. "What do you expect to find?" he asked softly.

She risked a look at him. She could detect his scent now, and she didn't like the effect it was having. "Elvis, of course."

He grinned. It was a painfully familiar flash of teeth, and it was enough to unnerve her. "Okay, dumb question," he admitted, sliding farther onto the bed. He settled back, his shoulder brushing hers. "Read it aloud."

"I wouldn't think you'd want to get involved with a ghost's problems," she countered, feeling a little winded.

"You've piqued my interest." He nudged her. "Read."

At the casual touch of his arm, a shuddery tremor rushed through her. She wanted to leap up and from a safe distance, scream for him to get out. But she resisted the urge. Logic told her that with his cop's instincts, he might see clues in the words that she'd miss. She cleared her throat and began, working at keeping her tone neutral.

Theora's narrative began on the eve of her marriage. At first the seventeen-year-old had seemed excited by her new position and wealth. She had money for all the dresses and jewels she could ever desire.

But not too many pages into the chronicle, her tone grew dispirited. Denby, her husband, was so very old— a man without his own teeth who bathed infrequently—and so domineering. Most upsetting of all and to her great dismay, old Denby had no talent at all in the bed chamber.

Alice's cheeks flamed as she read Theora's explicit descriptions of her husband's shortcomings and his "depraved" attempts to excite his young wife in bed. As she read, she had difficulty maintaining a composed facade. She wanted to squirm, for her thoughts were harking back to how well-satisfied Nick had left her when they'd indulged in some of the same acts Theora described with such disgust.

Nick made no comment, so she had no idea what he might be thinking or feeling. She wondered if his mind had drifted to the same place as hers. She was too cowardly to peek at his face, though, and just read on, hoping it would be over soon.

About midway through the book she came to a page that was splotched and smeared. "Oh, dear," she mused aloud. "She was crying when she wrote this."

"Try to read it," he prodded, his voice velvety and all too near.

She began haltingly, trying to piece the blurred narrative together. "'I have heard through Ada, the new kitchen maid, that Je—Je...'" She couldn't read the word.

"Jedediah." Nick leaned closer, his arm brushing against her breast as he pointed farther down on the page. "There it is again."

Alice cast him a sidelong glance. If he had the decency to be embarrassed, she couldn't see it in his face. Stifling a heavy sigh, she went on, "'Jedediah has left the village. Oh, my diary, when this news was delivered to me I felt it in my heart like a da—'"

"Dagger."

She turned toward him, her emotions frayed to the breaking point. "Do *you* want to read this?" she demanded impatiently.

He met her gaze, his brows furrowed, one corner of his mouth lifting in a quizzical smile. She sensed he thought she was acting very oddly. "I'm sorry," he said. "You're doing fine."

Calming herself, she found her place and read, "'I felt it in my heart like a dagger. I have come to realize that I made a grave error in judgment. When old Denby asked for my hand, I was blinded by all that I would have as his wife. The jewels and dresses and parties. I would be as a queen in the world. And I closed my heart to Jedediah's vow of love for me. Now he has left, and from what Ada has said, he has gone away because my marriage has broken his heart.'"

Alice swallowed to clear her emotion-clogged throat, then read on, "'As I sit in my golden castle, my diary,

I cry for the simple life and the simple blacksmith that I have lost because of my girlish wish for wealth and position. Now that I know the truth of it—that gold does not make happiness—I have no more wish to live upon this earth.

"'Forever I will mourn the loss of the good and kind man, who loved me, whom I cast aside with a laugh that last day we met in the meadow. My sweet Jedediah begged me not to wed old Denby. He sobbed as he vowed that he could offer me naught but his love as a sheltering tree in a stormy world. I recall his tears now with great pain in my heart. My wisdom has come too late, my diary. This day, I would gladly cast away my riches and be left with only my sheltering tree. But alas, he has gone away, to where I do not know—'"

Alice's voice broke and she couldn't go on. But it didn't matter. The puzzle was solved. Theora had decided she preferred security and respectability to a poor man's love. After discovering her mistake, she'd preferred to languish and die rather than live an empty lie. Now she roamed her lonely castle, cursed to search forever for her sheltering tree—her long-lost love.

Alice felt a rending pain in her heart, recognizing why she'd felt a kinship with Theora. They'd both been seduced by the same things—wealth and security—and they'd both imagined they were in love with men who represented that. And they'd both discovered later what real love was.

Yes, love was very like Theora's sheltering tree. She should have guessed what the ghost was searching for long before this. Nick had shown her by gently holding her in his arms whenever she was frightened or confused. She bit down on her lip. Ultimately, the learning had been a hard lesson.

Reluctantly she looked at Nick. He was watching her strangely. His gaze was so grave and intense she held her breath fearfully, waiting—but for what, she didn't know.

"Damn her," he whispered harshly, his nostrils flaring. "Damn that meddlesome bitch."

Alice was completely dumbfounded by his vehemence, but as she watched his grim profile, she began to understand his reaction. The truth about Theora had inadvertently brought home a painful truth to him— that a person's mistakes could damn them forever.

Nick's mistakes—or his guilt over perceived mistakes—had trapped him in a self-made emotional death, and he wandered the earth alone, without true fulfillment. He'd seen in Theora's fate a reflection of his own bleak future in a self-imposed hell. Though that was what he'd thought he'd wanted, and what he'd consciously chosen, the reality of it disconcerted him.

But Nick wasn't dead. His fate wasn't sealed. Any mistakes he'd made could be rectified. He only had to realize he wasn't responsible for what happened to his brother and his wife.

He'd turned away and was sitting on the edge of the bed, his fists clenched on his thighs. She felt a wrenching pain at the sight, for she loved a man who had decided not to love. But she realized that Theora's story had a message for her, too—which was not to let the one she loved slip away.

Feeling a new resolve, she moved beside him. "Nick," she began, touching his arm. "I've figured out a few things since I last saw you, and I understand now that you decided not to risk loving and then losing anyone else. So you don't get involved."

He didn't face her, but looked away toward the French doors where the day was quickly dying. A muscle in his jaw jumped, making it evident he didn't want to talk about this. "But, Nick," she forged on, even in the face of his torment. "Life has to be lived. You have to get involved. If you don't, you'll constantly be fighting your nature. You care—that's why you helped me."

For a split second he seemed to sag with defeat, then he straightened and looked at her, his eyes glistening with self-reproach. "Silvanus was a piece of slime."

"No," she objected. "That's not why you did it." As he warily eyed her, she continued. He was listening, possibly even beginning to face the futility of his choice. "You cared enough about me to risk everything—you jeopardized your career, your freedom, even your precious control when you brought me here." Her lips trembled with her gratitude and love. "You saved me from a terrible mistake. You couldn't help yourself— because you're a living, breathing man, Nick, not a heartless machine."

His face was almost too pained to look at, but she forced herself to hold his gaze, to make him confront this. "It's time for you to get on with your life, Nick. You must know by now that you can't avoid pain by trying to cut yourself off from people. And you can't control all the hurts of the world by carrying a gun."

She knew what she had to say, now. She knew it because Theora's story had told her she must. She was afraid, because what she was about to say would affect her whole life, her chance at true happiness. Yet it was a chance she had to take.

Awkwardly she cleared the lump of fear from her throat. "Nick, don't be afraid to reach out to someone. You have every right to be happy. What—" She lost her voice, and tried again. "What I'm trying to say is—I think you love me. I *know* I love you...."

It had come rushing out in a frail, breathy whisper. Feeling like a coward, she lowered her gaze, terrified of his reaction. She'd never done anything so outlandishly brazen in her life. It was up to him now.

She became aware of movement, then felt pressure on her arms as Nick touched her.

"You asked me earlier why I'd come back here," he said, his voice rough with emotion.

Lifting her head, she stared into his eyes. They were clouded with some emotion she couldn't name. When he spoke again, his mouth twisted in a rueful grin. "Maybe I came because I felt more at home with the damned." He paused, his troubled gaze raking her face. "Or maybe I came back because it was the only place I'd felt really alive in a very long time." As his eyes came to rest on hers, she thought she could see the sheen of something new in their green depths.

She caught her breath at the sight and hope began to rise within her. As soon as she saw it, she knew what it was. She was seeing the ghosts of guilt and fear leaving Nick's soul, like mist in the wind. She smiled tremulously at the beauty in his steady gaze, now devoid of the haunted sadness that had dwelled there for so long.

At that same moment there was a fluttering nearby, and they both stilled. Alice looked back at the diary she'd closed and set aside. It had opened, and the pages were fluttering, as if moved by a breeze. When they stopped, she watched wordlessly. Droplets of moisture seemed to erupt from the very paper.

"God," Nick murmured. "She's crying." He picked up the diary and brought it between them. It was open at the page Alice had just read.

"Look," she whispered in awe. "Every word has been smeared except in the two places where she wrote 'sheltering tree.'" She shook her head sadly. "She knows her sheltering tree is lost to her. I hope she can find peace, somehow."

Nick nodded, his expression solemn. Closing the diary, he silently replaced it in its hiding place.

Then there was a sigh of breeze that ruffled Alice's hair and a faint grating sound. They both turned in time to see the door key click into the locked position.

Nick chuckled deep in his throat, and Alice looked at him, her heart turning over. She could see something wonderfully alive in his eyes now, and it filled her whole being with joy.

"I think I forgive Theora for her meddling," he murmured. He reached for her then, and tenderly lowered her onto her back. He leaned over her, a lusty gleam in his eyes. "I seem to recall someone mentioning something about loving me? I think we should delve much, much deeper into that subject." He moved closer, his lips hovering near hers, his breath warm against her face. "There's such goodness in you, Alice, such beauty. I couldn't stay away from you, but you're right—I was afraid to feel. Now Theora hasn't given me any choice." His face was completely serious, and she could feel devotion in every word. "You might as well know this— I've loved you since the first moment I saw you."

Her heart thrilled. But then, as suddenly and painfully as a slap, she remembered her dark secret. Her smile faded and she turned her face away.

"What is it?" he asked.

She started to get up and move away, but he held her fast, repeating more urgently, "What's wrong? You do love me, don't you? Because I don't think I could survive losing you."

She shook her head. "Oh, Nick, I . . ." She couldn't go on. Squeezing her eyes shut, she turned her head back and forth, back and forth. He'd just declared his love for her, but—but he didn't know everything. There just wasn't an easy way to tell a man, who moments ago wanted no relationships at all in his life, that suddenly he'd not only committed to a woman but to a child, too. She decided there was no way to make it easy for him, so she simply blurted it out. "Nick, remember the last time we made love, and you forgot—we forgot—?"

"You're pregnant?" he interrupted, his voice low and concerned.

She felt a chill of dread and nodded. "I'm sorry. . . ."

"Oh, Lord." He pulled her to him with a relieved groan. "So much for my precious control." He kissed her temple, chuckling. "You certainly wreaked havoc on it."

She couldn't believe she was being cradled in his arms, and she stared up at him. She wanted badly to put her arms about his chest but resisted, still not quite ready to believe this could be happening.

"You weren't going to tell me, were you?" he admonished gently.

"I—I thought that was the deal."

He winced. "Hell." The curse was filled with self-reproach. "I wasted so many years being a frightened fool." His voice soft, he said, "I love children, Alice."

Everything inside her felt as if it had melted into one warm, mushy ball of joy. "I love you so much," she whispered, feeling an infinite peace envelop her heart.

Nick brushed her mouth with his, murmuring, "Someday I'll have to tell you how hot and bothered I get every time I read your sexy lips."

Laughter gurgled in her throat, and she teased, "That's not fair. You can read my lips, but I can't read yours."

His low chuckle mingled with hers as they relished their newfound completeness. Smoothing away a wisp of hair from her forehead, he kissed the place where it had been. "I promise," he assured tenderly, "you'll never have trouble reading my lips."

His tongue traced the full softness of her mouth, and she felt a shiver of anticipation. It was clear that his fears of involvement had truly vanished. He loved her as much as she loved him.

Thanks to Theora's ghostly interference, they would not make the same mistake she had.

Alice's body shuddered with delight as his lips found a sensitive place on her neck. "There's a great deal to be said for lipreading." She sighed. "I hope to become very good at it."

Moving lower and lower, driving her wild with pleasure, he whispered, "I have a feeling you'll become quite *gifted* that way, my love...."

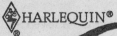

HARLEQUIN®

Temptation®

COMING NEXT MONTH

#513 HEARTSTRUCK Elise Title
The Hart Girls Book 2
Fired from her glitzy D.C. news anchor job and then dumped by
her "loving" fiancé, a downhearted Julie Hart slunk home to Pittsville.
The only job she could land was hosting "Pittsville Patter." Life was
the *pits*...until she met her gorgeous, blue-eyed, six-foot cohost,
Ben Sandler!

#514 A KISS IN THE DARK Tiffany White
For extra cash, Brittany Astor took an evening job reading aloud.
Only, her employer wasn't the sweet little old lady she'd imagined, but
notorious, sexy Ethan Moss—the man she'd been secretly lusting after
for years! He'd been temporarily blinded and needed someone to help
fill his time. For timid, plain Brittany, this was her chance to seduce
Ethan...but could she win him?

#515 LADY OF THE NIGHT Kate Hoffmann
Annabeth Dupree was *not* a call girl! Just because she'd inherited a
house of ill repute, didn't mean she'd reopened the business. So when
Zach Tanner threatened to have Annabeth arrested, she got mad. And
madder still when she realized she was falling for a man who thought
she was a fallen woman.

#516 THE BOUNTY HUNTER Vicki Lewis Thompson
Bounty hunter Gabe Escalante was hot on the trail of a dangerous criminal. When he suspected gorgeous Dallas Wade was the next target, he
vowed to watch over her. But soon Gabe wanted to be more than her
bodyguard. Not only her life was at stake now...so was his heart.

AVAILABLE NOW:

#509 DANGEROUS AT HEART
Elise Title
The Hart Girls Book 1

#510 PLAYBOY McCOY
Glenda Sanders

**#511 MOLLY AND THE PHAN-
TOM**
Lynn Michaels

#512 GHOST WHISPERS
Renee Roszel

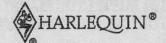

EDGE OF ETERNITY
Jasmine Cresswell

Two years after their divorce, David Powell
and Eve Graham met again in Eternity,
Massachusetts—and this time there was magic
between them. But David was tied up in a
murder that no amount of small-town gossip
could free him from. When Eve was pulled into
the frenzy, he knew he had to come up with
some answers—including how to convince her
they should marry again...this time for keeps.

EDGE OF ETERNITY, available in
November from Intrigue, is the sixth book in
Harlequin's exciting new cross-line series,
WEDDINGS, INC.

Be sure to look for the final book, **VOWS,** by
Margaret Moore (Harlequin Historical #248),
coming in December.

WED6

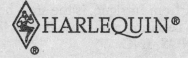

"HOORAY FOR HOLLYWOOD" SWEEPSTAKES

HERE'S HOW THE SWEEPSTAKES WORKS

OFFICIAL RULES — NO PURCHASE NECESSARY

To enter, complete an Official Entry Form or hand print on a 3" x 5" card the words "HOORAY FOR HOLLYWOOD", your name and address and mail your entry in the pre-addressed envelope (if provided) or to: "Hooray for Hollywood" Sweepstakes, P.O. Box 9076, Buffalo, NY 14269-9076 or "Hooray for Hollywood" Sweepstakes, P.O. Box 637, Fort Erie, Ontario L2A 5X3. Entries must be sent via First Class Mail and be received no later than 12/31/94. No liability is assumed for lost, late or misdirected mail.

Winners will be selected in random drawings to be conducted no later than January 31, 1995 from all eligible entries received.

Grand Prize: A 7-day/6-night trip for 2 to Los Angeles, CA including round trip air transportation from commercial airport nearest winner's residence, accommodations at the Regent Beverly Wilshire Hotel, free rental car, and $1,000 spending money. (Approximate prize value which will vary dependent upon winner's residence: $5,400.00 U.S.); 500 Second Prizes: A pair of "Hollywood Star" sunglasses (prize value: $9.95 U.S. each). Winner selection is under the supervision of D.L. Blair, Inc., an independent judging organization, whose decisions are final. Grand Prize travelers must sign and return a release of liability prior to traveling. Trip must be taken by 2/1/96 and is subject to airline schedules and accommodations availability.

Sweepstakes offer is open to residents of the U.S. (except Puerto Rico) and Canada who are 18 years of age or older, except employees and immediate family members of Harlequin Enterprises, Ltd., its affiliates, subsidiaries, and all agencies, entities or persons connected with the use, marketing or conduct of this sweepstakes. All federal, state, provincial, municipal and local laws apply. Offer void wherever prohibited by law. Taxes and/or duties are the sole responsibility of the winners. Any litigation within the province of Quebec respecting the conduct and awarding of prizes may be submitted to the Regle des loteries et courses du Quebec. All prizes will be awarded; winners will be notified by mail. No substitution of prizes are permitted. Odds of winning are dependent upon the number of eligible entries received.

Potential grand prize winner must sign and return an Affidavit of Eligibility within 30 days of notification. In the event of non-compliance within this time period, prize may be awarded to an alternate winner. Prize notification returned as undeliverable may result in the awarding of prize to an alternate winner. By acceptance of their prize, winners consent to use of their names, photographs, or likenesses for purpose of advertising, trade and promotion on behalf of Harlequin Enterprises, Ltd., without further compensation unless prohibited by law. A Canadian winner must correctly answer an arithmetical skill-testing question in order to be awarded the prize.

For a list of winners (available after 2/28/95), send a separate stamped, self-addressed envelope to: Hooray for Hollywood Sweepstakes 3252 Winners, P.O. Box 4200, Blair, NE 68009.

CBSRLS

OFFICIAL ENTRY COUPON

"Hooray for Hollywood"
SWEEPSTAKES!

Yes, I'd love to win the Grand Prize — a vacation in Hollywood —
or one of 500 pairs of "sunglasses of the stars"! Please enter me
in the sweepstakes!

This entry must be received by December 31, 1994.
Winners will be notified by January 31, 1995.

Name _____

Address _____ Apt. _____

City _____

State/Prov. _____ Zip/Postal Code _____

Daytime phone number _____
(area code)

Account # _____

Return entries with invoice in envelope provided. Each book
in this shipment has two entry coupons — and the more
coupons you enter, the better your chances of winning!

DIRCBS

OFFICIAL ENTRY COUPON

"Hooray for Hollywood"
SWEEPSTAKES!

Yes, I'd love to win the Grand Prize — a vacation in Hollywood —
or one of 500 pairs of "sunglasses of the stars"! Please enter me
in the sweepstakes!

This entry must be received by December 31, 1994.
Winners will be notified by January 31, 1995.

Name _____

Address _____ Apt. _____

City _____

State/Prov. _____ Zip/Postal Code _____

Daytime phone number _____
(area code)

Account # _____

Return entries with invoice in envelope provided. Each book
in this shipment has two entry coupons — and the more
coupons you enter, the better your chances of winning!

DIRCBS